THE ROYAL HOUSE OF NIROLI

Always passionate, always proud.

**The richest royal family in the world—
united by blood and passion, torn apart
by deceit and desire.**

Nestled in the azure blue of the Mediterranean,
the majestic island of Niroli has prospered for
centuries. The Fierezza men have worn the crown
with passion and pride since ancient times.
But now, as the king's health declines,
and his two sons have been tragically killed,
the crown is in jeopardy.

The clock is ticking—a new heir must be found
before the king is forced to abdicate. By royal
decree, the internationally scattered members
of the Fierezza family are summoned to claim
their destiny. But any person who takes
the throne must do so according to
"The Rules of the Royal House of Niroli."
Soon secrets and rivalries emerge as the
descendants of this ancient royal line vie for
position and power. Only a true Fierezza can
become ruler—a person dedicated to their
country, their people...and their eternal love!

The Official Fierezza Family Tree

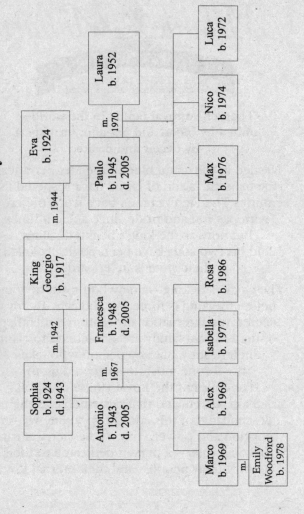

Melanie Milburne

SURGEON PRINCE, ORDINARY WIFE

THE ROYAL HOUSE OF NIROLI

Always passionate, always proud.

HARLEQUIN®

TORONTO • NEW YORK • LONDON
AMSTERDAM • PARIS • SYDNEY • HAMBURG
STOCKHOLM • ATHENS • TOKYO • MILAN • MADRID
PRAGUE • WARSAW • BUDAPEST • AUCKLAND

To Bev and Darrell Croker, thank you for being there
right from the start of this dream. Your continued belief in
me has carried me through some of life's toughest times.
Love you both.

ISBN-13: 978-0-373-38952-0
ISBN-10:   0-373-38952-3

SURGEON PRINCE, ORDINARY WIFE

First North American Publication 2007.

Copyright © 2007 by Harlequin Books S.A.

Special thanks and acknowledgment are given to Melanie Milburne
for her contribution to THE ROYAL HOUSE OF NIROLI series.

www.eHarlequin.com

Printed in U.S.A.

The Rules

Rule 1:   The ruler must be a moral leader. Any act that brings the Royal House into disrepute will rule a contender out of the succession to the throne.

Rule 2:   No member of the Royal House may be joined in marriage without consent of the ruler. Any such union results in exclusion and deprivation of honors and privileges.

Rule 3:   No marriage is permitted if the interests of Niroli become compromised through the union.

Rule 4:   It is not permitted for the ruler of Niroli to marry a person who has previously been divorced.

Rule 5:   Marriage between members of the Royal House who are blood relations is forbidden.

Rule 6:   The ruler directs the education of all members of the Royal House, even when the general care of the children belongs to their parents.

Rule 7:   Without the approval or consent of the ruler, no member of the Royal House can make debts over the possibility of payment.

Rule 8:   No member of the Royal House can accept an inheritance or any donation without the consent and approval of the ruler.

Rule 9:   The ruler of Niroli must dedicate their life to the Kingdom. Therefore they are not permitted to have a profession.

Rule 10: Members of the Royal House must reside in Niroli or in a country approved by the ruler. However, the ruler *must* reside in Niroli.

THE ROYAL HOUSE OF NIROLI

Always passionate, always proud.

Harlequin Presents is delighted to bring you a new series, THE ROYAL HOUSE OF NIROLI, in which you can follow the epic search for the true Nirolian king. Eight heirs, eight romances, eight fantastic stories!

The Future King's Pregnant Mistress
by Penny Jordan

Surgeon Prince, Ordinary Wife
by Melanie Milburne

Coming next:

Bought by the Billionaire Prince
by Carol Marinelli

Two of his heirs having been ruled out, the king turns to the black sheep of the family. Ruthless rebel Luca must forgo his lavish, decadent lifestyle and take his place on Niroli's throne.

The Tycoon's Princess Bride
by Natasha Oakley

Expecting His Royal Baby
by Susan Stephens

The Prince's Forbidden Virgin
by Robyn Donald

Bride by Royal Appointment
by Raye Morgan

A Royal Bride at the Sheikh's Command
by Penny Jordan

CHAPTER ONE

If SHE hadn't been running so horrendously late, she would never have taken the short cut in the first place.

Amelia let out a stiff curse as she tried to free herself from the rambling briar that had caught her as she'd climbed over the back fence adjoining the property of her last community health home visit of the day.

'Well, what do you know?' a deep male voice drawled from just behind her. 'The legend is true after all—there *are* fairies at the bottom of the garden.'

She swivelled her head around to see a tall man looking up at her where she was perched so precariously, his black-brown gaze twinkling with amusement.

It was very disconcerting as he looked so very Italian with his deeply tanned olive skin and his thick, short hair so dark, and yet she couldn't decide from his accent if he was American or British. He was even wearing what looked like an Italian designer shirt and trousers, the top four buttons of the shirt undone casually, leaving a great expanse of tanned, muscular chest on show.

'Is this *your* house and garden?' she asked, tugging at her lightweight cotton skirt to free it, with little success.

'No,' he said with a lazy smile. 'I'm just renting for a few weeks, but the landlord didn't tell me about the little bonus in the back garden. He should have charged me more rent. I would have gladly paid it.'

Amelia felt the colour begin to flare in her cheeks and, frowning at him, gave her skirt another little tug but it wouldn't budge.

His smile widened, showing very white teeth as his dark gaze ran over her appraisingly, taking in her petite shape and elfin features. 'Actually, I've changed my mind,' he said. 'You're not a fairy. You look more like a pixie to me.'

Amelia had to force herself not to roll her eyes at him in disdain. '*Actually*, I am a community nurse who is now more than half an hour late to visit an elderly patient,' she said through tight lips. 'And if you or your landlord took better care of your garden I would not be stuck up here like this!'

He folded his arms across his chest, rocking back on his heels as his eyes glinted at her playfully. 'And if you were not trespassing on private property you wouldn't have been ensnared by that bramble in the first place.' He unfolded one of his arms and waggled one long, tanned finger at her reprovingly.

She sent him an arctic glare and gave her skirt another vicious tug, but all she succeeded in doing was giving him a rather generous view of her thigh.

'If you tug any harder on that dress, you'll have me blushing to the roots of my hair,' he warned.

Amelia knew *she* was the one blushing to her backbone. She had never felt so embarrassed nor so annoyed in her life. 'Will you please leave me alone to extricate myself?' she clipped out. 'I would prefer not to have an audience right now.'

He put his hands up to his eyes. 'I promise not to peek.'

She let out a tight little breath and began to attend to her skirt, but she could feel those dark, laughing eyes watching everything from between his deliberately splayed fingers.

She finally tugged one part free of the bramble and shifted

position to attend to where her skirt had snagged on a nail on the fence.

'Can I look now?' the man called out.

'No,' she said, giving another forceful tug. There was a ripping sound and, before she could do anything to counteract it, she toppled down from the fence into the man's hastily outstretched arms below.

'*Oh!*' she gasped as he deftly caught her.

'Wow!' he said with a devilish grin. 'I haven't lost my touch after all. And here I was thinking that no woman was ever going to fall for me again.'

Amelia hastily pushed what was left of her skirt over her bare thighs, her face aflame. 'Please put me down,' she said as stiffly as she could, considering the sudden escalation of her pulse rate and breathing.

His face was so close she could see the black pupils of his eyes which were almost as dark as his irises. It looked as if his leanly chiselled jaw hadn't been anywhere near a razor for at least a day or two, but in spite of his lack of grooming she could smell the citrus fragrance of his aftershave mingled intoxicatingly with the muskiness of a man's body warmed by the hot spring sunshine.

He placed her on the ground in front of him, taking his time about it, she noted crossly.

'There, now turn around and let's see the damage,' he said.

Amelia stood completely frozen; she could feel air where she shouldn't be feeling air, and to make matters even worse—she was certain she was wearing her oldest pair of knickers.

'What's wrong?' he asked, but then, noticing the worried flick of her hazel gaze towards the fence, he whistled through his teeth and said, 'Uh oh.'

Amelia inwardly groaned as he walked up to the fence and removed what appeared to be the back half of her skirt from the nail. He came back and handed it to her, his mouth twitching at the corners. 'It might need a stitch or two, I'm afraid.'

'It's fine,' she said, backing away, doing her best to tuck the hapless bit of fabric into the elastic of the waistband of her skirt.

'Would you like me to give you a leg up over the fence?' he offered.

'No, thank you. I'll take the long way around.' She took a deep breath and picked up her bag with her free hand, the other one holding her skirt in place as she stalked back the way she had come with the precious little dignity she had left.

'Hey, you didn't tell me your name,' he called out after her, his mouth still tilted in a smile. 'Let me guess—is it Tinkerbell?'

She turned around and gave him one last cutting look. 'You do not need to know my name as I will not be coming this way again.'

'Pity,' he said, his eyes twinkling again. 'I kind of like the idea of having my very own pixie to play with.'

She stomped off muttering under her breath but the sound of his deep chuckle of laughter followed her all the way to Signora Gravano's house.

'You look like you have been through a hedge backwards,' the elderly woman said as she ushered Amelia into her neat little cottage.

'I have,' Amelia said, grimacing as she looked down at her tattered skirt, although she was relieved to find it had so far stayed in place.

'Did you take the short cut again?'

'Yes, unfortunately.' She gave the old woman a speaking glance and added, 'I met the new tenant.'

'Ah, yes, the associate professor. He just moved in this morning.'

Amelia's head jerked up. 'The associate *what?*'

'The Australian doctor,' Signora Gravano explained. 'I thought you knew about it. Dr Alex Hunter was summoned to Niroli to see the king about his heart. He very generously decided to use his sabbatical period to work with the Free Hospital staff to set up some sort of new heart procedure.'

'But he's not due until the end of next week,' Amelia said, her own heart suddenly feeling as if it needed an ECG. She turned to wash her hands to disguise her shock, taking her time with the soap and towel before she turned back round.

'I expect he has come early to enjoy the spring sunshine before he starts work,' the old woman said as she put her leg up on a foot stool for Amelia to inspect. 'It is quite a coincidence, don't you think?'

'Coincidence?' Amelia frowned in puzzlement. 'What do you mean?'

'He looks so Italian you could almost swear he was born and bred on the island.'

She frowned again as she turned back to her bag. 'I couldn't quite work out the accent,' she said as she opened her bag to retrieve the dressings she'd brought with her. 'I thought he sounded more British than anything.'

'He is very highly educated, of course. I believe he has spoken at conferences all over the world on this new technique. Perhaps his accent has become a little diluted by now.'

'So why is he renting that run-down cottage behind yours?' Amelia asked. 'If he's such a hot-shot doctor surely he would want to stay at Santa Fiera where the casino and all the resort hotels and restaurants are.'

'I suppose he wants to be close to the hospital and the older part of the island. Besides, he is only here for a month so a rustic working holiday might hold more appeal. The cottage is not that bad—it just needs a bit of a clean-up in the garden.'

There was no arguing with *that*, Amelia thought wryly, but

somehow she couldn't see the highly regarded cardiac surgeon getting down and dirty with a fork, spade and wheelbarrow.

'So what did you think of him?' Signora Gravano asked.

Amelia pursed her mouth as she unwrapped the old dressing on the old woman's leg. 'I thought he was…er…'

The old woman chuckled at her hesitation. 'He is very handsome, enough to make a woman's heart race, eh, Amelia? Good thing he is a cardiac specialist. He probably leaves a trail of broken hearts wherever he goes.'

'Yes, well, I am sure I will not be affected in such a way,' Amelia said firmly, doing her level best to block the memory of his strong arms around her.

'You have spent too long with the nuns,' Signora Gravano said. 'I always thought it would do more harm than good when you went to that convent after your mother passed away. You are too young to devote yourself to the sick without having a life of your own.'

'I do have a life of my own.'

The old woman grunted. 'You call that a life, living so far away in the foothills of the mountains like a peasant, cleaning up after your father and your brothers? You should be out dancing and enjoying yourself like other people your age. You work too hard, Amelia, far too hard.'

'I won't have to work so hard for ever. I've got a new job. I'm starting tomorrow.' Amelia straightened and added, 'The king needs a private nurse two days a week and I've landed the job. It fits in beautifully with my community work and my shifts at the Free Hospital.'

The old woman's grey brows rose over her black button eyes. 'What does your father think of you working for King Giorgio?'

'I haven't told him…yet.'

'Wise of you. Staunch Republican that he is, I do not think he would approve of you slaving at the Niroli palace.'

'I am thirty years old, Signora Gravano,' Amelia said. 'I

think I am old enough to work wherever I choose without the approval of my father or brothers.' She closed the bag with a little snap and added, 'Besides, my father is not likely to live much longer.'

'How is he?'

She let out a tiny sigh. 'Going downhill every day but he refuses to admit it. He won't go to the hospital and will not allow anyone to visit. Anyway, what doctor would travel all that way to see him only to be turned away? I do what I can but I fear it will not be long before he is beyond help.'

'Can you not convince your brothers to help you?'

'They help me when they can but they have struggles of their own. It is not exactly easy being a Vialli on the island of Niroli. Everyone has such long memories.'

'It was a terrible time on the island back then,' Signora Gravano said, her expression clouding. 'You are lucky you were not yet born. There was such hatred and violence, so much bloodshed.'

'I know…' Amelia released another sigh. 'My father's never really got over it.'

'There are many who believe he deserved to die as well,' Signora Gravano said with gravitas.

Amelia didn't respond, but she felt her blood chill just as it did every time she thought about the incident that had changed her family for ever.

'I must not keep you,' Signora Gravano said with a fond smile. 'You are a good girl, Amelia. Your mother would be very proud of you.'

Amelia bent down and gave the old woman a gentle hug. 'Thank you.'

'Why don't you leave your skirt with me to mend,' Signora Gravano offered as Amelia straightened once more. 'You can borrow something of my daughter's. She still has things in the wardrobe for when she visits.'

'I don't want to put you to any bother…'

'It is no bother,' she insisted. 'You are much smaller than her but it will see you home without embarrassment. You never know who you might meet and what would they think of you looking like a gypsy?'

A few minutes later Amelia looked down at the huge sack of a dress she had borrowed and wondered how she was going to walk the distance back to the Free Hospital in the stifling heat. Her brother Rico had yet again borrowed her car and had agreed to meet her back at the hospital once she had seen the last of the community patients.

She kept her head well down as she hurried past the visiting doctor's cottage, sure she could feel that dark, mocking gaze following her even though there was no sign of anyone about.

A flashy-looking sports car turned the corner and she stepped onto the grass verge to avoid its dust, but instead of going past it came to a halt beside her.

'Hey there, little pixie.' The man she had met earlier grinned at her through the open window. 'I see you've changed into something a little more comfortable.'

Amelia tightened her spine, her eyes flashing with sparks of ire. 'I believe you are the Australian doctor we have been expecting,' she said. 'What a pity you didn't think to introduce yourself properly when you had the chance.'

He turned off the engine and unfolded his long length from the car to come to stand in front of her. 'You didn't tell me your name so I didn't see why I should reveal mine,' he said with a teasing glint in his eyes. 'Fair's fair. It's my very first day on the island. A guy can never be too careful these days. For all I know you could be a dangerous criminal.'

She stared at him for a moment, wondering if he had heard the rumours about her family, her heart starting to clang like a heavy bell in her chest.

'You're not…' he bent slightly to peer deeply into her eyes '…are you?'

She took a little step backwards, almost tripping over the hem of the borrowed dress. 'W-what?'

'A dangerous criminal.'

'I—I told you before—I'm a…a nurse.'

His eyes flicked to her outfit before returning to her face. 'A plain-clothes nurse it seems. Are you on some sort of undercover operation?'

'I don't wear a uniform when I do my home visits,' she said. 'The patients feel less threatened that way.'

'Do you work at the Free Hospital as well?' he asked.

'Yes.'

'Which ward?'

She looked as if she had just bitten into a lemon as she answered, 'The cardiac ward.'

'Well, so we'll be work buddies, eh?' His dark eyes danced with merriment.

'It looks like it,' she said coldly.

He smiled down at her. 'So are you going to tell me your name or am I going to have to address you as Nurse Pixie for the rest of my stay?'

'Amelia Vialli,' she mumbled, but didn't offer him her hand.

'Alex Hunter,' he said and, reaching for her hand, held it in the huge warmth of his. 'How do you do?'

Amelia tugged at her hand but he didn't release it. She gave him a pointed glare but he just laughed. 'You can hardly rip half your arm off, now can you?'

'Are all Australians this rude or have you taken a special course in offending people?' she asked, wrenching her hand from his and rubbing at it with exaggeration. 'No doubt you passed it with flying colours.'

'And are all Niroli natives so unfriendly or is it just you?' he returned.

She scowled at him darkly. 'I am not being unfriendly.'

He grinned again. 'I'd hate to see you being hostile.'

'Excuse me,' she said and made to brush past. 'I have someone waiting for me.'

He stalled her with a hand on her arm. 'Would you like a lift?'

She sent him a haughty look as she brushed off his arm as if it were a particularly nasty insect. 'I don't think so.'

He raised his dark brows. 'You're going to walk all that way in that dress?'

She gave her head a defiant little toss. 'Yes.'

'What are you doing—moonlighting as a street sweeper or something?'

She rolled her eyes and swung away, and, picking up the voluminous skirt of her borrowed outfit, began to walk purposefully towards town, the fabric swishing around her ankles making her look like a small, angry black cloud.

Alex stood watching her, a little smile playing about his mouth. 'How cute is that?' he said out loud.

A light breeze carried the sweet fragrance of orange blossom and he closed his eyes and drew in a deep breath, relishing the fresh spring air after the long-haul flight from Sydney.

A whole month on the beautiful Mediterranean island of Niroli, by royal invitation no less.

Sure, there was a lot of work to do in a short time, but he would hopefully have enough free time available to explore the beaches and the nightlife, perhaps even do a hike up to the volcanoes.

Thinking of the volcanoes made him open his eyes to look back at the stiff little figure who was now almost at the end of the street.

He watched as a beaten-up car pulled up at the T-junction, a swarthy and scruffy-looking man in his early thirties opening the door from the inside so she could get in.

Alex blew out a long breath as the car rumbled on its way,

finally disappearing out of sight, although he could still hear it rattling and spluttering in the distance.

'Look's like she's already taken, mate,' he said as he turned back to his own vehicle and got back behind the wheel. He fired up the engine, giving it a few extra revs, and put it into gear. 'Now isn't that just the story of your sorry life?'

CHAPTER TWO

'How was your time at the palace with the king?' Lucia Salvati, the nurse on Amelia's afternoon roster, asked three days later.

'It was better than I feared,' she answered as she glanced at the patient list in the nurses' station.

'Why? Did he give you a hard time being a Vialli and all?'

Amelia shook her head. 'No. I don't think his bodyguards even mentioned my name to him. I just had to help him into bed and be on call in case he needed anything during the night. He barely addressed a single word to me the whole time I was there.'

'No wonder you look so tired,' Lucia said. 'Do you really have to take on this extra job? You already have enough on your plate with this place, not to mention the community work you insist on doing.'

'I've got nothing better to do. Besides, I need the money.'

'Don't we all?' Lucia groaned in agreement. 'Just wait until you're married with a couple of kids—that's when you'll be needing money and lots of it.'

'Yes, well, I'm not planning on getting married,' Amelia said with determination.

'Why? You're not still thinking of going back to the convent, are you? I thought you gave up on that idea—what was it…five or six years ago?'

'No, I'm not planning on going back. I just don't want the complication of a relationship,' Amelia said. 'I saw what it did to my mother—loving a man too much, losing her sense of self, her self-respect. I've decided I'd much rather be alone.'

'Your parents' situation *was* a little unusual,' Lucia pointed out. 'Besides, your mother wasn't to know what was going on in the background—hardly anyone did until it was over.'

Amelia released a heavy sigh. 'I know, but sometimes it seems as if the whole island would be happier if every one of us Viallis were dead and buried.'

Lucia gave her an empathetic look. 'Have your brothers been in trouble again?'

Amelia lifted her gaze to meet her colleague's. 'Rico lost his job at the vineyard. He got into a fight with one of the other workers. He wouldn't tell me what it was about but I can guess. It's always the same.'

'What about Silvio? Is he still employed down at the port?'

'I haven't heard from him for two weeks,' Amelia said. 'It might be because he has a new girlfriend or it might be because he's doing some underhand deal like the last time, which will no doubt bring even more disgrace to our family.'

'So you are working three jobs to keep food on the table,' Lucia said.

'What else can I do?'

Lucia gave her arm a little squeeze. 'You're right, there's nothing else you can do. I would do the very same but it seems a shame you are the one paying the biggest price.'

'My mother paid the biggest price, Lucia,' Amelia said as she got to her feet. 'She died because she fell in love with the wrong man at the wrong time.'

'How is your father?'

'As difficult as ever.'

'You still can't convince him to have treatment?' Lucia asked.

'He hates doctors. Ever since he was diagnosed with cancer

he won't have anything to do with anyone medical, apart from me, of course, but even with me he's becoming increasingly uncooperative.'

'Speaking of doctors, have you run into the Australian yet? Word has it he's come a few days early to get a feel for the island before he meets the king. Apparently this new technique could be the answer to the king's heart problem. At ninety years of age a triple bypass is terribly risky, but Dr Hunter has pioneered this off-pump bypass procedure. It's apparently much less traumatic than being cooled on bypass and having your heart stopped, especially for older patients.'

'I can't see it ever happening at this hospital,' Amelia said, carefully avoiding answering Lucia's original question. 'We haven't got the beds for one thing, and we're constantly short-staffed.'

'The king will no doubt insist on having it done at the private hospital, but Dr Hunter has come to train the cardiac team here. I think it's very good of him to give up his time. He could just as easily have refused and gone off to sun himself before returning to Sydney. We should do all we can to support him while he's here.'

Amelia shifted her gaze and began to shuffle some papers on the desk in front of her. 'I'm thinking about a transfer to another ward.'

'*What?*' Lucia's tone was incredulous. 'You can't be serious! But you are cardiac trained.'

'I know, but I feel like a change.'

'But that's crazy, Amelia. You'll be needed more than ever with Dr Hunter here. It would be embarrassing if we were short of cardiac nurses to help with the recovery of the patients he's operated on.'

'There are other nurses who could do the job.'

'That's not true. We're chronically under-staffed, and, besides, you know you are the most experienced nurse amongst us. You can't possibly consider leaving us in the lurch like that.'

Amelia chewed at her bottom lip. She knew Lucia was right, but the thought of seeing that seductive smile across a patient's bed was unthinkable. It was cowardly, but she didn't have the aplomb to follow through from such a mortifying first encounter.

'Don't tell me you have something against Australians,' Lucia filled the tiny silence. 'Practically half of us on Niroli have relatives living over there. Besides, from what one of the other nurses said Dr Hunter looks more Italian than anything else.'

'Yes, I know,' Amelia said with a little frown. 'I thought so too when I met—'

'*You've met him?*' Lucia's eyes bulged.

'Er…yes…'

'So what's he like? Does he say "G'day, moite" and "crikey" and stuff like that?'

Amelia couldn't help laughing at her friend's attempt at an Australian accent. 'No, he sounds…' she suppressed a tiny shiver as she recalled that deep velvet voice '…well educated and…'

'And?' Lucia prompted eagerly.

'He's…very strong.'

'Strong?'

'As in big muscles,' she explained with heightened colour.

Lucia's brows rose slightly. 'So how did you get to see the size of his muscles?'

Amelia gave her a wry look. 'Believe me, you don't want to know.'

'Oh, but I *do*!' Lucia called after her as Amelia left the nurses' station. 'You'll have to fill me in sooner or later!'

Amelia opened her mouth to politely tell her to mind her own business when she caught sight of a tall figure striding down the corridor towards them with Vincenzo Morani, the senior cardiac surgeon, by his side.

'Ah, this is the nurse I was speaking to you about,' Dr Morani said as they drew closer. 'Amelia, this is Dr Alex Hunter from Australia. I have been telling him you are our most experienced cardiac nurse, one of our most valuable assets in post-operative care.'

Amelia stretched her mouth into what could loosely be described as a smile. '*Buongiorno*, Dr Hunter.'

'We've already met, haven't we?' Alex said with a cheeky grin that crinkled the corners of his dark-as-night eyes.

'Oh?' Dr Morani looked faintly relieved. 'Well, then…I'll leave you two to have a chat while I get organised for Theatre.' He turned back to Amelia. 'You don't mind showing Dr Hunter around the rest of the department, do you? I have an urgent matter to see to in ICU.'

'But I—' She stopped when she saw the look Alex Hunter gave her.

'Don't tell me you're embarrassed about our meeting the other day?' he asked in a gravelly undertone once the other surgeon had left.

'Of course not,' she lied. 'It could have happened to anyone.'

'Anyone wearing a dress that is.'

She turned from his teasing look and began quickly striding up the corridor reciting mechanically, 'This is the nurses' station and over there is the tea room and over there is the storeroom for the—'

'What are you doing tonight?' he asked.

Amelia stopped in her tracks and gaped up at him. 'I beg your pardon?'

'I've seen so many hospitals in my time I'm sure I'll be able to find my way around this one without a guided tour. What I would prefer is if you would show me around the island.' He gave her a little wink. 'How about it?'

She struggled to get her voice into gear. 'I—I don't think that is such a good idea.'

'I'm sure your boyfriend won't mind if you tell him it's work-related,' he said.

'I do *not* have a boyfriend.'

His eyes lit up. 'Great, then it's a date. I'll pick you up. Where do you live?'

She glanced up at him in alarm. 'I am not going anywhere with you.'

He gave her a mock-forlorn look. 'Hey, just because I saw your knickers the other day doesn't mean I want my wicked way with you. I just want you to show me around.'

'Find someone else,' she bit out frostily, her colour at an all-time high as she resumed stalking down the corridor. 'I'm not interested.'

Alex smiled to himself as she disappeared around the corner.

He had a month to change her mind.

Amelia had arranged for Rico to pick her up after her shift was finished, and he was in another of his foul moods.

'Hurry up. I've been waiting for twenty minutes,' he growled as she got in the car.

'Sorry, I had to spend some time with the relatives of a patient,' she said. 'Is *Papà* all right?'

His mouth twisted as he put the car into gear. 'You're not going to believe this but he wants to see a doctor.'

She swivelled in her seat to gape at him. 'Really?'

He flicked a quick glance her way. 'I couldn't believe it myself but he insists he wants to see the new doctor.'

Amelia felt her stomach drop. 'The Australian one?'

'Yes. He thinks he of all people will not be biased against him.'

She let out a prickly breath. 'Dr Hunter is a cardiac surgeon, Rico, not an oncologist. There's no cure for lung cancer, or at least certainly not for the stage *Papà* is at. He's coughing blood every day and the original cat-scan showed the rapid expansion of the tumours and—'

'He wants to see him and he wants you to arrange it as soon as you can.'

She sat back in her seat, a hollow feeling settling in her stomach. Her father needed palliative care, not a social call from a visiting heart specialist who was the biggest flirt she had ever met. Well, maybe not quite the biggest flirt, she thought bitterly. Even now, eleven years on, she still couldn't help that empty sinking feeling whenever she brought Benito Rossini's features to mind. She had been a fool to fall for his easygoing charm, not for a moment stopping to think if the handsome businessman visiting Niroli from Milan was already taken. It had devastated her to find he had a wife and two children at home. She had given him her innocence and he had betrayed her in the worst possible way.

'Have you heard from Silvio?' Rico disturbed her painful reverie.

'No... I just hope he's not doing anything illegal,' she said, looking out at the grey-green of the olive groves they were passing. 'I couldn't bear it if we had something else to live down.'

Her brother gave a rough grunt. 'As soon as I get some money together I'm going to leave the island. I am tired of living with the shame of the past.'

Amelia turned to look at him. 'But what about *Papà*? Surely you're not thinking of leaving before he...' she hesitated over the word '...goes.'

He lifted one shoulder dismissively. 'It's his fault we have been forced to live this way.'

'That's not true!'

Rico sent her a cynical glance. 'You are just like *Mamma* was, too innocent to see the truth until it was too late.'

She frowned at his tone. 'What do you mean?'

'There are things about *Papà* you should know.'

Amelia felt her throat tighten. 'W-what sort of things?'

'Things about his role with the bandits thirty-four years ago.'

'He wasn't a key person. *Mamma* told me he got caught up in it but had never intended to play a major role. He's told me that himself, and I believe him. Think about it, Rico. Our father is a bit rough and unpolished around the edges, but he's not a violent man. He has never raised a hand to any of us— how can you possibly think him capable of condoning the activities of such a despicable movement?'

'There are rumours circulating on the island that he had something to do with the kidnapping of the infant prince,' he said.

Amelia felt her heart begin to pick up its pace at the grim expression on her older brother's face. 'There have always been stupid rumours. It doesn't mean you have to believe them.'

'But what if someone has irrefutable proof of his involvement?'

She stared at him, shock rendering her speechless.

He met her eyes briefly. 'You have heard that Prince Marco has renounced his right to the throne once King Giorgio abdicates?'

'Yes…I have heard about it,' she answered.

Marco Fierezza's parents and his uncle had been tragically killed two years ago in a yachting accident, which had left him as the next in line after his grandfather, King Giorgio. There had been some speculation about the nature of the accident, some people suggesting it had been yet another attempt to bring the monarchy down, but so far no evidence had been brought forward to convict anyone of anything untoward. The coroner had made his decision that the yacht had come to grief as a result of the wild storms that had ravaged the coast of Niroli that year and which had been fiercer than ever before.

The island had lately been buzzing with the news that Marco had decided to marry his mistress, Emily Woodford, a young Englishwoman, who—because she had been previously divorced—made it impossible for Marco to claim his right to the throne.

Amelia had thought it incredibly romantic that a man would give up his birthright for the love of a woman. Renouncing the throne of Niroli, with its long and ancient history, must have been a huge decision for Prince Marco. And a sacrifice she was sure few modern men would be prepared to make.

The Fierezza family had ruled the island since the Middle Ages, and with its rich volcanic soil and temperate climate the island had prospered as a key port on a major wine, spice and perfume trading route. But while the island of Niroli was ruled by the monarchy headed by the ageing and increasingly unwell King Giorgio, the neighbouring island of Mont Avellana was now a republic partly due to the resistance movement that had occurred in the nineteen seventies.

Amelia was well aware of the ongoing resentment and rivalry between the two islands and often wondered if her younger, somewhat wayward, brother Silvio was in some way involved in a resurgence of the movement that had cost both the monarchy and her family so dearly.

'King Giorgio is becoming impatient to find a contender for the throne,' Rico said. 'His fading health makes it imperative he does so soon, otherwise the continuation of the monarchy could be under threat.'

'I suppose that's why he invited the Australian specialist all this way to see him,' Amelia said with a cynical twist to her mouth. 'I wonder how much he paid him.'

Rico gave her a quick sideways glance. 'The doctor would not accept payment of any kind.'

She stared at him again. 'How do you know?'

'I have it on good authority that Dr Hunter refused all

offers of money from the king. He came to the island because he is keen to bring this new technique to less affluent hospitals around the globe. He agreed to meet the king and give his professional opinion on his condition and whether he would be a suitable candidate for the surgery, but apart from that he insisted he spend the majority of his time at the Free Hospital and that any donations made go towards its upkeep.'

Amelia sat back in her seat with a little frown pulling at her forehead. She felt a little ashamed of her too hasty assessment of Alex Hunter as an opportunistic playboy on a royally funded visit. If what her brother had said was true, the visiting specialist had similar goals to her own—bringing a much better standard of care to the patients who couldn't afford the expense of private health care.

But he was still an outrageous flirt, she reminded herself in case she was tempted to recall again the feel of those strong, muscular arms around her. The last thing she needed in her life was a man with a smile that could melt a glacier.

'You said someone has proof about *Papà*'s involvement with the rebellion,' she said. 'What sort of proof?'

'There is talk that the infant prince who was kidnapped wasn't actually killed.'

Amelia gave him an incredulous look. 'But that's crazy, Rico. I walked past the little boy's grave the other day at the palace.'

He sent her a quick unreadable glance. 'A child was certainly killed during the rescue operation, but what if it isn't Prince Alessandro Fierezza that is buried at the castle?'

Amelia felt a shiver run from the base of her spine to disturb the tiny hairs on the back of her neck. 'What are you saying? That *Papà* was somehow involved in this?'

'You said it yourself. *Papà* is not a violent man. What if he couldn't go through with the orders he was given by the leader of the bandits and spirited the prince away instead of killing him?'

She frowned as she considered the possibility. 'But a child *was* killed.'

'Yes, that's true.'

'But not necessarily by *Papà*...'

'You still want him to be innocent, don't you?' he asked.

'I can't bear the thought of our father killing an innocent child, prince or not,' she said. 'He just couldn't possibly have done such a thing.'

'The rumours are not going to die down. It will make life even more difficult for us on the island.'

'Is that why you lost your job at the vineyard?' she hazarded a guess.

'I was going to leave anyway. I am sick of being treated like a peasant.'

'You should have stayed at school like *Mamma* wanted. You would have had more choices in terms of a career.'

'Like you, you mean?' he said with a cynical movement of his lips. 'At least I have some sort of life.'

'I wish people would not keep criticising me for choosing to care for others instead of myself,' she grumbled. 'I love my work. It fulfils me.'

'You don't have to give your life away in order to serve others.' He threw another quick glance her way. 'Once *Papà* dies you will be free to do what you want with your future. You could even leave the island, go and work in some other place for a while. It would make you realise there is a whole world outside of Niroli.'

Amelia knew there was an element of truth in what he said. She had cloistered herself away for too long, but the alternatives were just too threatening. She was frightened of making another dreadful mistake. She didn't have the experience that other women her age took for granted. She had only had one lover and it had turned her world upside down. The lingering shame of it still clung to her like a scratchy fabric against her tender skin. How had she been so blind, so gullible and so trusting? She just didn't know how to relate to men other than as patients or relatives, and as for her medical colleagues—she kept them at a professional distance at all times.

It was safer that way.

'I will need the car again tomorrow,' Rico said as he took the turn to their run-down cottage in the foothills. 'I have some business to attend to. I can give you a lift to the hospital but I think I should warn you I am leaving before sunrise and I might not be back until midnight.'

'I'll take the pushbike,' she said, her heart sinking at the thought of the long ride into town. At least most of the journey was downhill, but the return trip after a day on the ward was no picnic.

'Maybe you could ask Dr Hunter to give you a lift home tomorrow,' Rico suggested. 'That way you can kill two birds with one stone.'

'I hardly think Dr Hunter is going to make a house call way up here,' she said. 'I'll try and convince *Papà* to see him at the hospital or even the community clinic.'

'He won't go. You'll have to get the doctor to come here. I am sure he won't mind. Perhaps you could offer to show him around the island as a return favour—he probably won't expect payment.'

Oh, yes, he will, Amelia thought as she brought that sensual smiling mouth to mind. 'I'll see what I can do, but I'm not making any promises,' she said.

Rico sent her one of his rare smiles. 'You're a good sister, Ammie. I don't know what we would do without you.'

She smiled back at him shyly. It was indeed a rarity to receive a compliment from either of her brothers and certainly never from her father. 'Thank you, Rico. I just want us all to be happy and free of the past.'

The smile instantly faded from her brother's face. 'We can

never be free of the past. It has cast a shadow over us that will not go away.'

Amelia followed him into the cottage with a despondent sigh. She hated to admit it but her brother was right.

What the nuns had taught her was true: the sins of the fathers were revisited on the next generation.

All her life she had lived with the burden of being a Vialli, the most scorned and hated family on the island of Niroli for what they had done to the king's little grandson.

She suppressed a little shudder at the thought of that tiny broken body buried in the palace grounds, the Fierezza coat of arms emblazoned on his headstone, the family motto inscribed below.

Sempre Appassionato, Sempre Fiero.

Always passionate, always proud.

She had stood in respectful silence that day, comforting herself that at least the little prince was now at rest with his parents in heaven.

But what if he was still alive as her brother had suggested, but totally unaware of his royal heritage?

And if he was indeed alive, then who was the little boy who now lay in the Fierezza family vault…and why hadn't his real parents come forward to claim him?

CHAPTER THREE

'THERE'S a parcel for you in the third drawer of the filing cabinet,' Lucia said on Amelia's arrival at the hospital the next morning.

'A parcel?' Amelia wiped her damp face with a tissue. 'For me?'

Lucia looked up from the notes she was writing. 'You look like you've just run a marathon. Has Rico taken your car again?'

Amelia nodded and tossed the tissue in the bin under the desk. 'His is still in the workshop. They won't release it until he pays the bill, but I can't see that happening too soon now he's out of work. I had to use the pushbike.'

'You should have called me. I could have taken a detour to pick you up.'

'And add to your already frantic morning getting the children off to school and your husband off to work? No, the exercise will do me good. I quite enjoyed it actually.'

'I'd offer to run you home but I've already promised the girls I'd take them swimming at the beach after school.' Lucia gave her an apologetic look.

'I'll be fine,' Amelia assured her. 'Anyway, Rico might make it in time to pick me up.' She opened the drawer and took out the neatly wrapped parcel and stared at it for a moment.

'Aren't you going to open it?' Lucia asked.

She turned the package over in her hands and frowned. 'It doesn't say who it's from.'

'Go on, open it. It's addressed to you.'

Amelia undid the slim ribbon before unpicking the tape holding the brightly coloured wrapping in place. The paper fell open to reveal a beautiful summer dress in three bright shades of pink, the skirt soft and voluminous, the fabric exquisite to touch.

'Wow!' Lucia breathed a sigh of wonder. 'Someone has very good taste. If I'm not mistaken, that looks like a Mardi D'Avanzo original.'

Amelia checked the label on the collar of the dress, her heart giving a sudden lurch as she saw the famous Italian designer's name printed there. 'It is…'

Lucia's eyes twinkled. 'So who is your admirer? It's not your birthday for months.'

Amelia carefully rewrapped the dress, scrunching up the little card she'd found inside the wrapping. 'Is Dr Hunter in yet?' she asked.

Lucia leaned forward in her chair, her eyes going wide. 'Did Dr Hunter buy that for you?'

Amelia straightened her spine resolutely. 'Yes, and I am giving it back to him right now.'

Lucia looked confused. 'How come he bought you a dress?'

'I'll tell you later. Where is he?'

'I think he's in the office Dr Morani organised for him. But aren't you being a bit hasty? I mean, that's a designer outfit!'

Amelia gave her a determined look. 'I can buy my own clothes. I am not going to accept his or anyone else's charity.'

She strode down the corridor and gave the office door a couple of hard raps with her knuckles.

'Come in,' Alex called out cheerily.

She opened the door and closed it behind her with a little snap and locked gazes with him where he was sitting behind his desk.

'What is the meaning of this?' she bit out, thrusting the parcel at him.

He got to his feet and smiled. 'Did you like it? I kind of had to guess your size but you're about the same size as my younger sister Megan.'

Amelia slapped the parcel on the top of his desk. 'I cannot accept this from you,' she said, her tone crisp with pride.

'If you don't like the colour I can always change it,' he offered.

'It's got nothing to do with the colour!' she said, only just resisting the urge to stamp her foot at him.

'Then what's the problem?' he asked.

'You had no right to buy me this.'

'On the contrary, I thought I had a perfect right to do so,' he said, his dark eyes running over her lazily before returning to her fiery gaze. 'I was partly responsible for you ruining your dress the other day, so I thought it was the very least I could do to replace it.'

'With this?' She pointed to the parcel on his desk.

He rubbed at his cleanly shaven jaw for a moment, his eyes still holding hers. 'Mmm…now what did I get wrong? It must be the size. I know women absolutely hate it when the men in their lives get their size wrong.'

'You did *not* get the size wrong and I am *not* the woman in your life.' This time she did stamp her foot. 'I just cannot accept such an expensive outfit from you or indeed from anyone.'

'I thought the colour would bring out the raven's wing darkness of your hair.'

She glared at him without answering.

'It's meant to be a compliment,' he explained. 'You have the most beautiful, shiny hair. It was the first thing I noticed about you when I saw you perched on the top of my back fence.'

Amelia fought against the compliment's effect on her feminine psyche but it took a huge effort. Her hair was cut short, she did nothing to it but wash it each day. She couldn't remember anyone ever calling it beautiful before, or at least not in a very long time.

'It makes you look like an elf,' he added with a tilt of his mouth.

She gave him a scornful look. 'I thought you said I looked like a pixie?'

He grinned down at her. 'Pixie, fairy, elf—what's the difference?'

She pursed her mouth at him. 'A pixie has funny ears.'

'Show me your ears,' he said.

She stepped backwards. 'I—I beg your pardon?'

He stepped forwards. 'Go on. Prove to me you're a pixie not an elf. I dare you.'

'This is a t-totally ridiculous c-conversation,' she said and backed away even farther, but she came up against the closed door. She had to crane her neck to keep eye contact, her heart skipping as fast as a professional boxer in training.

'W-what are you doing?' she squeaked as his hand reached for her hair.

She shivered all over as his fingers tucked her hair behind one of her ears, his touch so gentle it felt like a caress of a long, soft feather against her sensitive skin. She couldn't get her lungs to inflate properly and all of a sudden she had an almost uncontrollable urge to drop her gaze to the sensual curve of his mouth...

'Well, how about that?' he said as he stepped backwards. 'I was wrong. There's absolutely nothing weird about your ears.'

Amelia was completely lost for words. She opened her mouth a couple of times but nothing came out.

She watched as he walked back over to his desk, his long legs encased in dark trousers that highlighted his lean, athletic build. His light blue shirt was rolled back at the cuffs, revealing his tanned wrists with the sprinkling of dark masculine hair running down his arms to the backs of his fingers. He was wearing a silver watch—she couldn't make out the brand but she assumed it was worth a small fortune.

She stiffened as he picked up the parcel but instead of handing it to her he pulled out the bin from beneath his desk and dropped it into it.

'What are you doing?' she blurted, pushing herself away from the door.

He gave her a guileless look. 'I'm throwing the dress away.'

'B-but...*but why?*'

He gave a loose shoulder shrug. 'You don't want it.'

'But that doesn't mean you have to throw it away! You can give it to someone else...your sister, for instance.'

'I bought it for you, not my sister,' he said. 'And besides, how would you feel if a guy bought a present for another woman and ended up giving it to you?'

'Um...'

He gave her a knowing little smile. 'See? I told you. You wouldn't like it one little bit.'

Amelia's eyes went to the bin and she swallowed. 'I—I could find someone who would really like it...I mean...rather than you throw it away...'

'Oh, would you?' He gave her a grateful smile. 'I'd really appreciate it. It cost an absolute packet—not that I mind, of course, as I can afford it—but my parents always taught me to be responsible with money. What's that old saying? If you look after the pennies the pounds look after themselves?'

Amelia was starting to think Alex Hunter had far too much talent in the way of charm. She could feel her mouth twitching and had to bite her tongue to stop herself from laughing out loud. No man, not even Benito with his silver tongue, had had this effect on her.

He handed her the parcel, his fingers brushing against hers. 'Please try and find it a good home,' he said soberly. 'I was getting very attached to that dress.'

A burst of laughter spilled from her mouth. She tried to cover it with a cough, but she could see he wasn't fooled.

He gave a huge grin and raised his closed fist in the air in a punch of victory. 'I knew I could do it!' he crowed delightedly.

'D-do what?' She tried to restrict her smile but her mouth wouldn't cooperate.

'I wanted to make you smile and I did it. I had my doubts there for a while, but I finally wore you down.'

'You're impossible,' she said and turned to leave, a ridiculous smile still stuck on her face.

'Hey, are we still on for a date some time?' he called out as she got to the door.

She turned around to look at him. 'I can't possibly go on a date with you,' she said, her belly doing a funny little flip-flop as she met his eyes once more.

'Why not?'

She hunted her brain for a valid excuse. 'I…I have nothing to wear.'

His gaze went to the parcel under her arm before returning to hers, a smile tilting up the corners of his mouth. 'You could always wear that, but to tell you the truth, I really liked the one you had on the other day.'

She frowned at him in puzzlement. 'The long black one?'

He shook his head. 'No, the one with the great view.'

Amelia could feel the colour firing in her cheeks and wished she had more poise to deal with his effortless charm and playful banter.

'I have to go…' She reached for the door with clumsy fingers, her heart fluttering like a confined sparrow.

'Here.' He reached past her shoulder and opened the door for her. 'Allow me.'

She breathed in the fragrance of his aftershave, its citrus grace notes making her senses whirl all over again at his closeness. 'Th-thank you.'

He waved her through gallantly. 'It was so nice of you to call round to see me,' he said with another stomach-flipping grin. 'Feel free to drop around any time.'

She shook her head at him and left, but it took most of the morning before she could wipe the smile off her face, and even longer before the mad fluttery sensation in her stomach died down to a soft little pulse....

CHAPTER FOUR

IT WAS a punishing ride home. Amelia gave the hot sun a resentful scowl as she pedalled up the hill, certain it had come out in full force just to make her journey all the more tiresome.

It had been a long day. One of the cardiac patients had taken a turn for the worse and she'd had to deal with distressed relatives who wanted a miracle to happen when a lifetime of bad diet and bad habits had led to the damage in the first place.

She hadn't run into Alex Hunter since she'd gone to his office. She'd heard he was taking the registrars through the procedure in a workshop prior to a case organised for Theatre the following morning.

Somehow she had fielded Lucia's questions when she'd come back to the ward, giving her a cut-down version of what had happened when she'd first met the visiting specialist.

Amelia felt a little guilty that she hadn't yet asked Alex about her father's request to see him. She knew her father would question her as soon as she returned for news of when he would come to visit, but somehow the thought of Alex seeing where she and her family lived embarrassed her. He was clearly very wealthy—how would he react to entering a cottage that hadn't seen a brush of paint in close to twenty years? The furniture was threadbare and mostly unstable, the floorboards rickety and the curtains at the windows let more light in than they kept out. Spiders had taken up residence in every corner in spite of her best efforts to keep them at bay, and the hens that fought over every last crumb in the yard had made what was left of her mother's garden a pock-marked wasteland.

She sighed as she forced the stiff pedals around yet another time, sweat breaking out on her upper lip at the effort.

'Vialli villain!' a youthful voice called out from the grass verge as a rock flew past her ear.

She flinched and wobbled on her bike, but somehow managed to keep it upright. She turned her head to see who had thrown the rock, but whoever it had been had run off.

It wasn't the first time she'd encountered missiles along this section of the road that led to the cottage; over the last few months some of the local youth had taken it upon themselves to regenerate the hostility of the past, more from mischief, she imagined, but it didn't make it any easier to cope with.

She pedalled on, gritting her teeth for the next hill when another rock flew past her head. This time the bike tilted and she lost control, tumbling off to land in the gravel on the side of the road.

It was all she could do not to cry. She got to her feet with an effort and righted her bike, but the fall had punctured the front tyre. She looked around but there was no sign of anyone to help. She was at least ten kilometres from the cottage and it was uphill all the way.

She brushed at her dusty face and plodded on, the parcel containing the dress Alex Hunter had given her strapped to the rack on the back of the bike.

After fifteen minutes or so she heard the sound of a powerful car coming up the hill behind her. She moved to the side of the road, her shoulders hunched as she pushed the bike through the loose gravel, the perspiration stinging as it streamed past her eyes.

'Hey there, little elf.' A familiar voice spoke from the open window of the car as it pulled up alongside her. 'You look like you need a lift.'

Amelia's bottom lip wobbled dangerously as she turned to look at Alex Hunter. 'I—I'm fine, thank you,' she said, somehow summoning up a tattered remnant of pride.

His playful smile disappeared to be replaced by a frown. He killed the engine and got out of the car to take the bike from her. She tussled with him for a moment before finally letting it go, her hands going up to her face to cover the shame of her tears.

'Oh no,' he said softly, and, putting the bike to one side, gathered her up against his broad chest, his deep voice rumbling against her breasts where they were crushed up against him. 'What on earth is the matter?'

'I—I have a p-puncture…and s-someone threw a rock at me,' she sobbed.

She felt him tense against her. 'A rock? What sort of rock?' he asked.

'I don't know… It was probably just a pebble…' She gave a little sniff. 'It happens now and again…'

He held her from him to look down at her, his expression serious. 'What do you mean it happens now and again?'

She brushed at her eyes with the back of her hand. 'It happens a lot. They're just kids making mischief. It's because of my family's history…. It's too hard to explain.'

'The Vialli bandits?'

She looked up at him in surprise. 'You've heard of them?'

He nodded. 'I've been reading up on the history of the island. It's quite a colourful past.'

A shadow came and went in her eyes. 'Yes, well, if only people would leave it in the past where it belongs…'

'So you're a relative of the original Vialli gang?' he asked.

'Yes and no. My father was only on the fringe of the operation. He wasn't directly responsible for anything that happened,' she explained.

'So who was the ringleader?'

'One of my uncles,' she said. 'He was killed during the takeover bid, along with several other relatives. My father has been made the scapegoat for the last thirty-four years. He virtually lives the life of a hermit to keep away from the past.'

'That's tough,' Alex said. 'What about your mother?'

Amelia bent her head to stare at the front of his shirt where her tears had left a damp mark. 'She died when I was eighteen. It broke her heart living up here away from all her family who had turned their backs on her.'

'So what actually happened?'

'It's a long story.'

He gave her an encouraging smile. 'I love long stories.' He led her to the grassy verge away from the dusty gravel. 'Here, sit down and tell me all about it.'

Amelia sat next to him on the cushion of grass so they could face the view as she related the story, hastily covering her scratched and dirty knees with her uniform. She could feel his broad shoulder close to hers and her nostrils flared again to breathe in the alluring scent of his maleness.

She took and a breath and began, 'Well…the Vialli bandits were originally ex-Barbary corsairs.'

'Pirates, huh?'

'Yes, amongst other things. Anyway, they formed a resistance to overturn the monarchy. They kidnapped one of the king's twin grandsons and demanded a ransom. The king refused to pay it.'

Alex frowned. 'Why did he do that?'

'I don't know.' She glanced at him briefly, her teeth capturing her bottom lip for a moment before she released it and turned back to look down at the lush valley below. 'Maybe he didn't want to be seen being manipulated or something.'

'So the kidnappers killed the little prince?'

She hesitated for a fraction of a second. 'Yes…his body

was found after an undercover rescue attempt failed. He had
been blown up by a bomb.'

She felt Alex wince. 'Hard to live down that sort of
stuff,' he said.

'Yes.'

'So what was left of your family has had to live with that
ever since?' he asked.

'Yes. It's been hard…you know…everyone looking at you
as if you have murder and insurgence on your mind,' she said
with a dejected slump of her shoulders.

'Poor little elf,' he said, turning her head so he could cup
her face as he looked into her eyes. 'It sounds to me as if you
need to be taken away from all this drama for a while. Are we
still on for dinner?'

'D-dinner?' She looked at him with a shadow of uncer-
tainty in her green-flecked hazel eyes.

'Yes, that's why I came up here in the first place. One of
the nursing staff said you lived up here in the foothills. I was
taking a chance on finding you at a loose end so I could take
you out to dinner somewhere.'

'There aren't any restaurants up here.'

'I know, but what about down at Porto di Castellante?'
he suggested.

Amelia lowered her gaze, frightened of the temptation
he was dangling before her and even more terrified she
wouldn't be able to resist it. 'I have to cook my father
something….'

'I heard he's not well and not keen on seeing anyone professional,' Alex said. 'I thought if I came up to take you out
it might be a way of breaking the ice in case there's anything
I can do for him.'

She raised her gaze back to meet his, a look of surprise
flickering there momentarily before she looked away again.

'Did I say something wrong?' he asked.

'No…it's just that he asked me to ask you to visit him, but I just didn't get around to it when I…er…saw you earlier today.'

'I can't promise to be of any help but sometimes it helps to get a second opinion.'

'He's got advanced lung cancer,' she said, the bleak resignation evident in her tone. 'A second opinion is not going to save him.'

'That's sad,' he said. 'What about palliative care? Who is overseeing that?'

She let out a defeated sigh. 'He won't accept any treatment.'

'So you are managing him on your own?'

'Not very well, I'm afraid,' she confessed, her eyes drifting to the view once more. 'I have tried my best to get him to be reassessed but he won't budge. He's not in much pain as yet but I dread what is ahead.'

'It's a brute of a disease,' he said with feeling. 'I'll have a chat with him and see if I can change his mind. Besides, we can always organise some self-administered morphine for him to use at home when things start to go downhill.'

'You're a heart specialist,' she said, looking at him again. 'This is not your responsibility.'

'Perhaps not, but how else am I going to get you to agree to come out with me?' he asked with a twinkling smile.

Amelia felt the familiar kick of panic deep in her stomach. She had travelled this road before and it had almost ruined her life. Alex Hunter was here for work and pleasure; there was no promise of permanency. How could there be? She would be a fool to even dare to dream otherwise.

'You're only here for a month,' she reminded him, a tight set to her mouth.

'So?'

'So…that's not long enough to get to know someone properly.'

'Listen, Amelia, I'm an open book. What you see is what

you get. I'm not hiding any dark secrets. I'm not married and nor am I currently involved with anyone and haven't been for quite some time.'

'So that's supposed to reassure me?' she asked with a deepening frown.

He smiled at her. 'Of course.'

Amelia felt herself caving in in spite of her every attempt to counteract it. He was so utterly charming and irresistible. What would it hurt to go on one little date with him? she wondered. The fact that he was only here for a short time made it even less likely for her to be in any danger of losing her head or heart, she reasoned. Besides, this was a chance for her to prove to herself once and for all she had moved on after her experience with Benito. Only a naïve fool would fall into the same trap twice and she was no fool, or at least not any more.

Besides, Lucia and her brother were right—she *did* need to have a bit of a life now and again. All work and no play was a sure-fire recipe for burn-out and then who would look after her father and brothers?

'I don't know…' she began hesitantly, not wanting him to see how tempted she really was.

'Come on, give me a chance. I promise not to step over any boundaries. No sex, well…not on the first date anyway, but after that who knows?' He gave her another teasing grin.

She gave him a school-mistress look. 'You really are incorrigible.'

'I know, but you're so cute I can't resist trying to win your heart.'

'It would take a whole lot more than a sexy smile and a quick wit to win my heart,' she said, trying to purse her lips but failing hopelessly.

'You think I've got a sexy smile?' His eyes glinted as they held hers. 'I have to confess I've had extensive orthodontic work done.' He tapped his two front teeth. 'These are totally fake—porcelain veneers. I had my teeth knocked out during a football match.'

There was nothing she could do to stop her smile. 'You really are unbelievable.'

He tapped her on the end of her nose. 'So are you, elf.' He got up and pulled her to her feet beside him. 'Now, come on—let's get this poor bike in the back of my car and get you home and hosed, and ready for our first date.'

Amelia sat in the front seat of his car as he loaded her bike in the back and mentally prepared herself for the first time he saw the poverty of her home. She could already feel herself cringing in shame. It had been years since she had brought anyone to the cottage. She always arranged to meet the few friends she had kept over the years at their homes, or at a quiet café well away from the main centres of the island.

'It's this turn here on the left,' she directed him after they had gone a few kilometres, a fluttering sense of nerves assailing her the closer they got. 'I'm sorry the road is not in better condition. Your car will be filthy.'

'No problem.' He sent her another one of his high-beam smiles.

She took an unsteady breath and looked forwards once more. 'It's very good of you to come up here like this...but I must warn you it's probably nothing like you're used to.'

Alex concentrated on negotiating the rough driveway that led to a dilapidated cottage in the shelter of the trees. He could sense her embarrassment and wondered how he could put her at ease. He'd seen his share of poverty-stricken homes during his various field trips to less developed countries, and knew how important it was to not jeopardise someone's sense of dignity just because they didn't live in a house that met the western standards he'd grown up with and more or less taken for granted.

'It must be really peaceful living way up here,' he commented as he parked the car underneath one of the trees.

'Yes…it is.'

He came around and opened her door for her, frowning when he saw her scraped knees as she got out of the car. 'You've hurt yourself. Why didn't you tell me? I could have done something earlier.'

'It's nothing…just a scratch.' She brushed her uniform back down over her legs.

'I've got my doctor's bag in the back. I'll dress those grazes for you now.'

'No, please…it's fine…really. I have my own first-aid kit things inside.'

He didn't press the issue; instead he followed as she led the way to the cottage, but he noticed how her brow was furrowed and her shoulders slightly hunched as if she carried a too-heavy weight on her back.

Amelia opened the front door but there was no sign of her father when she entered the cottage. *'Papà?'* she called out.

Alex came up behind her. 'Has he gone out?'

She frowned as she led the way inside. 'He hardly ever goes out.'

She looked around the kitchen where the dishes her father had used that morning were still on the table. Her gaze went to a note propped up against a mug. It was in her father's roughly scrawled handwriting informing her he'd gone somewhere with Silvio and would be back late and not to worry.

'What does it say?' Alex asked.

She folded the note and pocketed it, a shadow of unease in her hazel eyes as they met his. 'My younger brother has taken him somewhere.'

'Is that unusual?'

'No…not really, except Silvio hasn't been home or even in contact for two weeks…' A small frown tugged at her smooth forehead.

'Maybe he's taken your father out for a meal or something.'

She nibbled at her bottom lip for a moment. 'Maybe.'

'Well, look on the bright side,' he said. 'You don't have to cook dinner for him after all.'

'But you came up to see him and now he's not here.'

'I can come some other time,' he said. 'It's no trouble.'

'Maybe something's happened.' Her frown deepened. 'What if he's taken a bad turn?'

'Then your brother will take him to the hospital. Why not call the switchboard and ask if he's been admitted?' he suggested.

A tide of colour washed into her cheeks and Alex mentally kicked himself. Of course she couldn't call the hospital. There was no electricity that he could see or any sign of a telephone. He could only assume she wouldn't have the funds available for a mobile either. He reached for his own mobile. 'I'll give them a quick call myself. What's his first name?' he asked.

'Aldo,' she answered, twisting her hands together.

He made the call and after a brief conversation replaced the phone in his pocket. 'No, he hasn't been admitted.'

She blew out a tiny breath. 'I can't help worrying about him.'

'That's understandable, but at least he's with your brother so you can take the rest of tonight off and kick your heels up with me.'

She gave him an apologetic glance. 'I don't think I should go out tonight. I'm sorry.'

'I'm not taking no for an answer,' he said. 'You deserve some time off. A quick dinner by the seaside will be good for both of us. Besides, I gave you a lift home so you owe me.'

Amelia could tell by the determined look in his eyes that she was going to have a hard time convincing him to leave without her. The thought of spending the evening alone in the cottage wasn't too appealing, but she felt she should at least put up a token resistance. 'I don't know…I have an early start tomorrow.'

'No earlier than mine. Come on, get a wriggle on. We're

wasting valuable time here when we could be sitting watching
the sun go down with a glass of wine in our hands.'

She could feel herself weakening. 'I need to freshen up
first. Do you mind waiting?'

'I don't mind at all,' he said, and pulled out a chair and sat
down. 'I've got a couple of calls to make anyway. I'm
expected at the castle tomorrow evening. I guess there's some
sort of protocol I'm meant to follow. I don't suppose I can turn
up there and slap the old guy on the back and say, "G'day,
mate, I'm Alex Hunter." I'd better check with the castle staff
on how I'm supposed to address him.'

Amelia fought back a wry smile as she left him busily
punching in numbers. She was certain he knew exactly how
to address anyone from royalty to the lowliest commoner
without turning a single hair. He hadn't given any sign of
being put off by the run-down nature of her family home,
which made it all the harder for her to keep him at a relatively
safe distance. Most men would have turned up their noses and
backed out without even bothering to say goodbye. Her ex-
lover, Benito, had been appalled by the distance he'd had to
travel to pick her up, let alone the condition of the cottage
when he'd got there. He had made her feel so ashamed, and
in her youth and innocence she had failed to see the warning
signs that their relationship was not as it should have been.
But perhaps she hadn't wanted to, she thought with a little
pang of sadness as she moved towards the cramped bathroom.

After a quick, cold bath because there wasn't time to heat
water on the fuel stove, she spent ten minutes agonising over
what to wear. Her choices were limited to start with, but she
finally narrowed it down to the dress Alex had bought her or
a skirt and blouse that had belonged to her mother. However,
her mother's outfit was ruled out as soon as she put it on. It
had faded over time and did nothing for her, hanging off her
slight frame like a sack.

With almost reverent fingers she picked up the dress Alex had bought and slipped it over her head, gently doing up the zipper at the side. She twirled in front of her mottled mirror, amazed at how the beautiful fabric brought out the creamy tone of her skin and the green flecks in her hazel eyes.

She rummaged in her small supply of cosmetics and found a lip-gloss and applied it to her mouth, wondering what the nuns at Saint Gregorio's would say if they could see her now.

Then, giving herself one last twirl, she picked up her only evening purse and went back to where Alex Hunter was waiting for her, a tiny, moth-like fluttery sensation in the middle of her stomach at the thought of being alone with him for the rest of the evening.

CHAPTER FIVE

'I'VE changed my mind,' Alex said, getting up from the chair as she came back to the kitchen. 'You're not an elf or a pixie—you're a princess.'

Amelia knew her cheeks were glowing but there was nothing she could do to disguise it. 'It's a beautiful dress,' she said softly. 'Anyone would look like a princess in it.'

'Do you think you should leave your father a note in case he gets back before you do?' he asked.

She nodded and, quickly scribbling a message on the back of the note her father had left, she propped it up against his mug again.

Alex escorted her out to the car, shooing the hens away from her as they went. 'Make way for Her Royal Highness Princess Amelia,' he said. 'Come on, ladies, be off with you.'

Amelia giggled as the hens scuttled off with ruffled feathers. 'They're not all ladies,' she said, pointing to the proudly strutting rooster amongst them.

'Sorry, mate,' he addressed the rooster. 'I didn't see you there.' He turned back to Amelia and grinned cheekily. 'What a life he must have, all those ladies to himself with no competition.'

Amelia felt her cheeks grow warm as she thought about how many women had flown in and out of his life. His playboy lifestyle afforded him numerous opportunities to flit from one relationship to the other, and with his easy charm and unmistakable sexual potency she began to realise she was in very real danger of joining their number.

Alex tipped up her chin with one hand while he used the other to graze his knuckles over the bright pool of colour on her cheek. 'Do you know you're the first woman I've been able to make blush in years?'

She looked into his dark eyes, her pulse beginning to race as his knuckles caressed her again. Her heart felt as if it were growing in size, her legs as if they had been disconnected from the bones that were supposed to hold them upright.

'I—I'm not used to this sort of thing,' she said, her tongue sneaking out to unconsciously moisten her mouth.

'What sort of thing?'

'Flirting, joking, dating…that sort of thing.'

He looked puzzled for a moment. 'How old are you?'

Her cheeks fired up again. 'Thirty.'

'Then you really have to make up for lost time,' he said, and, stepping away from her, opened the car door. 'I've got a whole six years on you.'

Amelia waited until they were on their way before speaking again. 'I suppose you are very experienced in the ways of the world and find me something of a novelty.' She hadn't really intended to sound quite so priggish but it was too late to take the words back now.

'To tell you the truth I find you delightfully refreshing,' he said, sending her a quick glance, the white slash of his smile devastatingly attractive against the olive tone of his skin.

'But you're laughing at me all the same. I can tell.'

'That chip on your shoulder will ruin that dress by stretching it all out of shape,' he warned her playfully.

'I haven't got a chip on my shoulder.'

Alex flicked another glance her way and skilfully redirected the conversation. 'You have two brothers, right? What do they do for a living?'

She let out a little sigh. 'Rico, my older brother, recently lost his job at one of the vineyards. He hasn't had a lot of luck with steady employment. Silvio, my younger brother, has been even worse. He's been restless most of his life, flitting from one thing to another. He's employed down at the main port but he doesn't really talk about what it is he actually does.'

'I guess that puts an extra strain on you,' he said.

'It does.' She looked down at her hands in her lap. 'I've had to take up some extra work…at the palace.'

She felt his gaze swing her way. 'Doing what?' he asked.

'Nursing the king two nights a week.'

'So what's the old guy like?' he asked.

'His bodyguards don't really encourage conversation with him,' she said. 'Besides, I prefer to play a low profile.'

'Because of your family's history?'

'That and…other things,' she said, tucking a strand of hair behind her ear self-consciously.

'You're not intimidated by all that monarchy stuff, are you?' he asked, swinging another quick glance in her direction.

She met his eyes briefly. 'So you're not a monarchist yourself?'

He gave a little noncommittal shrug. 'It's an ongoing debate in Australia about whether we should become a republic. I haven't really made up my mind. Too busy saving lives I guess.'

'Your work is very demanding,' she said, releasing a tiny breath to counteract the effect of his close proximity. 'It's a wonder you had the time to come over here to help our people.'

'When I received a royal summons I was a bit intrigued, I can tell you,' he said. 'I had heard about the island before but, while it was somewhere on my list of must-see places, I wouldn't have come right now, but my parents were keen for me to do it.' He sent a quick smile her way and added, 'I guess they want to dine out on it a bit. "Have we told you about our son who mixes with Italian royalty?" That sort of thing goes down a treat at a dinner party.'

'But you're not fazed by it all—or, if you are, you're not showing it,' she surmised.

'I'm a doctor, Amelia. My first priority is to heal the sick and if I can do that in a way that helps the underprivileged then I'm more than happy. Don't get me wrong, I come from a wealthy background which has given me some wonderful privileges, but my parents have always encouraged both Megan and I to give something back to the community and not just our neighbourhood one.'

'Your family sounds wonderfully supportive,' Amelia said, thinking sadly of all she had missed out on in hers.

'They are. I am very lucky.'

'How old is your sister?' she asked after a little silence.

'She's twenty-five.'

'That's quite an age gap between you—eleven years,' she observed.

'I know, but it was a long time after my adoption papers were processed before they could adopt another child,' he said.

Amelia swung her gaze to look at him again. 'You're… you're adopted?'

'Yes, and very proud of it.' His dark eyes met hers briefly. 'My adoptive parents are fabulous people. I owe them a great deal. When you think about it, I could have ended up with much worse.'

She waited until he'd brought the car to a stop outside one of the restaurants in Santa Fiera before asking, 'Have you ever thought of tracing your biological parents?'

He met her gaze across the small width of the car. 'Now and again I've thought of it but I haven't done anything about it. I guess my main reason has been to save my adoptive mother the hurt she might feel if I were to go looking for the woman who gave birth to me. It's a sensitive subject. My adoptive mother was unable to have children of her own. She grieved terribly that she couldn't give my father what he most wanted. Of course, the reproductive technology available today would have solved her problems in an instant. But she is the only mother I've ever known, even though I was what was considered in those days a late adoption.'

Amelia felt the small silence begin to tighten the air in her chest. 'How late?' she asked, glancing at him.

'I was two years old.'

A tiny shiver passed over the back of her neck, lifting each and every fine hair. 'So…so you don't recall anything at all of your infancy? I mean, before you were adopted?' she asked.

He answered her question with a question of his own. 'Tell me, Amelia, what's your very first memory?'

She thought about it for a moment. 'I was about three, I think, when my mother made me a fairy dress with wings on the back of it. She told me later how she had made it from the material of her wedding dress and veil. I can't really remember anything before that.'

'That's about average for most people. Neurological studies have shown that the infant brain is not mature enough to store reliable memories until about the age of three.'

'What about in terms of emotional and physical abuse?' she asked. 'Surely if the infancy was traumatic enough there would be some trace of it in the child's later behaviour?'

'Perhaps, but that would not necessarily be because the child actually remembered what had happened, but more of an instinctive feeling in an evolutionary sense that life was unsafe and chaotic during that time.'

Amelia mused over his answer as they walked into the restaurant. They were led to a table near the windows that overlooked the beach of the main tourist area, which had been recently developed on the island, the casino, restaurants and health spa attracting large crowds during the spring and summer months.

The waiter handed them menus and the wine list and left them alone to decide.

'What wine do you recommend?' Alex asked, looking at the list in his hands.

'I'm not much of a wine connoisseur but the Porto Castellante Blanco is known as the signature wine of the island. The Niroli vines have been cultivated since Roman times,' she said, recalling what Rico had told her while he had been working at the vineyard. 'It's said that the Niroli vines produce the queen of white grapes.'

'Let's give it a go, then,' he said, and signalled to the waiter.

Amelia tried to relax as their wine was poured a short time later but she was way out of her comfort zone and felt sure it showed. She glanced at the other couples and parties dining and wished she could appear less gauche, but she had so rarely eaten out and was terrified in case she picked the wrong piece of cutlery.

Alex picked up his glass and raised it in a toast against hers. 'Here's to mending the broken hearts of Niroli.'

She lowered her gaze for a moment, a shadow passing over her features.

'What's wrong?' he asked.

'Nothing.'

'Confession time, little elf.' He reached across the table and tipped up her chin with his finger, his dark eyes meshing with hers. 'If you tell me who broke your heart I'll tell you who broke mine.'

'I can't imagine you having your heart broken,' she said, her gaze slipping away from his to stare into the contents of her glass.

'It happens to the best of us, believe me,' he assured her

as he leaned back. 'My work gets in the way a lot. I guess that's why I've reached this age without settling down.'

'Is that what you want to do some time? Settle down?' she asked, taking a tentative sip of wine.

'I don't know.' A small frown brought his dark brows closer for a fraction of a second. 'I thought I wanted to once but it didn't work out.'

Amelia wondered if she'd been wrong about assuming his heart was unbreakable. He acted like a carefree playboy, but she couldn't help wondering now if it was a cover-up for deeper hurt.

'What about you?' he asked, his expression lightening once more. 'Are you like most other young women living in hope that Prince Charming will come along one day and sweep you off your feet?'

She gave him a twisted smile as she reached for her wine again. 'It's a nice fantasy, but hasn't anyone told you there aren't enough princes to go around?'

He smiled back at her. 'You could always settle for an ordinary bloke. How about me? Want to run away and get married and have my babies?'

Amelia's mouthful of wine burst from her mouth and sprayed across the table to pepper the front of his shirt. She gasped and choked and died a thousand deaths of embarrassment, but all he did was hand her his napkin and chuckle with amusement.

'I think I must have jumped the gun a bit. Maybe I should have kept that for our second date.'

'I can't believe you *said* that…' She glanced around to see if anyone had seen her mortifying moment, but to her relief no one had appeared to, or if they had they were too polite to stare. She brought her gaze back to his. 'You're joking…right?'

He leaned forward again and took one of her hands in the warmth of his, his dark gaze holding hers. 'What if I wasn't?'

She pulled her hand out of his, her mouth tightening with reproach. 'Please don't make fun of me. I might not have the experience of other women my age, but I'm not a complete fool.'

'I had no intention of making fun of you. It kind of slipped out. I didn't even know I was going to say it until the words were out of my mouth—honestly.'

She gave him a hardened little glare. 'I know what you're up to but it won't work with me. You're only here for a month and you're looking for a playmate to pass the time.' She got to her feet and thrust her napkin on the table. 'Go and find someone else to warm your bed. I'm not interested.'

Alex gave the waiter a handful of notes and brushed past the other diners to follow her, finally catching up to her a couple of blocks down the street. 'Amelia, listen to me.'

'Go away.'

'Damn it, will you stop walking so fast and listen to me for a minute?'

She swung around to face him, her chest heaving, her eyes flashing with green and brown sparks of fury. 'You really take the prize for the biggest ego. I thought my first lover was bad, but you surpass him in spades.'

He stood watching her without speaking, a small smile tipping up the edges of his mouth.

'Stop looking at me like that.' She glared at him crossly.

'Like what?'

'You keep smiling at me.'

'You make me want to smile.'

'I don't want you to smile at me.'

'Then you're going to have to stop doing that.'

'Doing what?'

'That little thing you do with your mouth.'

She scowled at him. 'What little thing?'

He took her hands in his and pulled her up against him.

'That pursed-lipped thing. You do it all the time. It drives me crazy. It makes me want to kiss you.'

'That's…that's ridiculous,' she said, staring at his mouth.

'Is it?' He pressed a hand to the small of her back and brought her even closer.

'O-of course it is.… You hardly know me.…'

'I know. It's never happened like this before.'

'I don't believe you. You're just saying that to tempt me into allowing you to kiss me.'

'Is it working?'

'Is…is what working?' She was still staring at his mouth, her gaze mesmerised by its sensual contours, made all the more captivating by the gentle curve of his smile.

He lowered his head until his lips were so close to hers they almost grazed them as he spoke. 'I've wanted to kiss you from the first moment I saw you on my back fence.'

Amelia knew if she moved her lips to form a single word the battle to keep him at bay would be lost. She stood, totally transfixed, her body tingling all over at the feel of his pressed so closely, his maleness against her femaleness, his muscular strength against the yielding softness of hers.

But then, almost without her realising she was doing it, her tongue sneaked out to moisten her lips and involuntarily brushed against his bottom lip, sending sparks of electricity right through her.

'You really shouldn't have done that, little elf.' This time his lips did graze hers, his warm wine-flavoured breath mingling with her quickly expelled one.

'I—I didn't mean to do that…' she breathed, her lips buzzing with sensation as they moved against his.

He pressed a soft, barely touching kiss to her mouth. 'Sure you did.'

'No…' She kissed him back, softly, shyly. 'No…no…I didn't.…'

He smiled against her lips, making them instantly vibrate with intense longing. 'You're lying to me. You really want to kiss me. I can tell.'

'No…it's you that wants to kiss me.'

He lifted his head a fraction, just enough to meet her gaze, his eyes dark and gleaming with desire. 'You're right. That's exactly what I want to do.'

Amelia watched as his gaze dipped to her mouth, the thick black lashes fanning down over his eyes, his head coming down…

'Wait!' She placed her flattened palm to his chest.

He lifted his head to look down at her. 'What's the matter?'

'We're standing in the middle of the street,' she whispered as some people strolled by.

'Are we?'

'You know we are.'

He looked down at her mouth again. 'I forgot about that.'

She gave a small, embarrassed laugh. 'Just as well I reminded you. We could have made complete fools of ourselves.'

'I guess we'll have to do this some other time, then.'

'I guess.'

He held her gaze for a long moment without speaking.

'I'm sorry about dinner,' she began awkwardly. 'I shouldn't have rushed out of the restaurant like that.'

'We can always go back in and start over,' he suggested. 'I'm sure the waiter won't mind. Besides, I'm starving.'

'So…shall we do it?' she asked after a tiny pause.

'Do what?' he said, looking at her mouth again.

'Go and have dinner.'

'Oh, I thought you were talking about the other thing.'

She wrinkled her nose at him. 'What other thing?'

'This other thing,' he said, and before she could do a thing to prepare herself his mouth came down and set fire to hers.

CHAPTER SIX

AMELIA felt the full-throttle passion of Alex's kiss in every nerve and cell of her body, leaving her starved senses reeling. His tongue was slow and languorous at first, but then as if fuelled by his growing desire it became more demanding, drawing hers into a mutual sexy tango that sent lightning bolts of feeling to her toes and back. She could feel his reaction to her against her stomach, the rapid thickening of his body reminding her of how very powerful human desire was and how easily it could slip out of one's control.

She fought against her own response but her body seemed to have a mind of its own, unleashing a wild and uncontrollable urge to feel more and more of his touch. It made her press closer and closer against his hardness, her breasts swelling as if reaching out to him for his intimate attention, her skin prickling with the need to feel his body move and slide against hers.

She felt the moistening of her feminine core where the pulse of desire was already drumming a primitive beat low and deep inside her, her whole body humming with an escalating need she had never experienced in such an out-of-control way before.

She heard him groan, a deep, guttural, almost primal sound that rumbled against her breasts and fuelled her reaction to him until she forgot they were standing in full view of the public.

One of his hands cupped her cheek to angle her head for deeper access, his other hand in the small of her back to press her even harder against him.

He was incredibly aroused, the length of him surprising her even though she wasn't completely without experience.

The sound of voices and footsteps approaching must have jolted Alex into awareness of where they were as he suddenly pulled away, and, giving her a quick, almost self-conscious grin, ran a hand through his hair in a distracted manner. 'Now *that* is what I call a kiss. Where'd you learn to do that?'

She gave him a flustered look. 'Um…I…'

He smiled and, tucking her arm through his, escorted her back to the restaurant. 'Never mind—I don't think I really want to know. I might start to feel jealous.'

They were soon re-seated at the same table and the waiter refreshed their glasses with the chilled wine. Food orders were taken and fresh crusty bread and a little plate of warmed marinated local olives appeared.

After their main course was set before them Amelia found herself finally beginning to relax, the wine easing a bit more of her tension with every sip she took. Alex had done his best to put her at ease, chatting in his easygoing manner to her about his work and how he hoped to train the cardiac team at the Free Hospital, but, even so, every now and again her mind kept drifting back to that explosive kiss. She could still taste him in her mouth and her lips felt swollen and overly sensitive each time she sipped her wine. She could even feel the hard, warm presence of his legs beneath the table; once or twice as he shifted in his chair they brushed against hers, unleashing a shock wave of awareness through her lower body.

Alex reached across to refill her wineglass, his dark eyes meeting hers. 'How is your meal?'

'It's wonderful,' she said, sending him a shy smile. 'I haven't been out to dinner for years.'

His eyebrows lifted. 'How many years?'

She ran a fingertip around the rim of her glass, her eyes watching the movement of her finger rather than meet the dark probe of his gaze. 'Eleven.'

He whistled through his teeth. 'That must have been one hell of a bad meal you had way back then.'

She felt a reluctant smile tug at her mouth as she lifted her eyes to his. 'It was. I got my heart broken for dessert.'

'Not a good way to end a meal or a relationship.'

'No.'

Their gazes locked for a moment and then, as if in unison, slowly lowered to each other's mouths, the air suddenly charged with erotic possibilities.

Alex was the first to break the spell. 'So what happened?' he asked, reaching for his wine.

'I was too young and inexperienced to see the signs. I had not long lost my mother and was feeling a bit rudderless. A handsome man visiting the island paid me a lot of attention and I stupidly fell for it,' she said, trying not to let her gaze drift back to the warm temptation of his.

'A handsome married man, I suppose,' he commented.

'Yes, very much so.' She let out a tiny sigh. 'He had two little children back in Milan. Their photographs fell out of his wallet when he dropped it. I picked it up and of course he had all the usual excuses—my wife doesn't understand me, we no longer have a physical relationship, blah, blah, blah.'

His dark gaze softened with concern. 'How did you cope?'

She brushed her hair back with a soft movement of her hand, her cheeks going a delicate shade of pink. 'I got myself to a nunnery.'

He gave her an incredulous look. 'You're kidding, right?'

'No.' She toyed with the rim of her glass with her fingertip again, her expression clouding briefly.

'Were you going to take vows?'

'I was seriously considering it.'

'What changed your mind?'

She gave him a wry smile. 'The vow of chastity wasn't really hard for me, but the vow of silence was.'

He laughed. 'Yeah, I can see how that might have been a problem for you.'

'It was. I had a tendency to answer back, which didn't go down very well.'

'So you left and took up nursing?' he said.

'Yes, I wanted to do something with my life, something for other people instead of hiding away in a convent.'

'Not all nuns hide away in convents,' he pointed out. 'I've worked with several who were teaching or nursing in some of the developing countries I'd visited.'

'I know, but I missed my father and brothers after three years. I decided I could do more good on Niroli by working at the Free Hospital as well as one or two community shifts.'

'You weren't tempted to take your skills to the private hospital where the pay would be better?' he asked.

'No, never. I think it's terribly unfair that the well-to-do have top-quality health care while the poorer members of our community have to do with second best.'

'It's a real problem in most developed countries,' he said. 'Those who can afford private health cover often need it less than those who can't.'

'So that's part of the reason you are here, isn't it?' she asked. 'Apart from the royal summons, of course.'

'Yes, I thought it would be a good opportunity to train the cardiac team while I was here on sabbatical. Vincenzo Morani in particular is keen to learn the technique.'

'You're employed at a teaching hospital in Sydney?' she said, this time unable to keep her gaze from tracking back to the warm intensity of his.

'Yeah, I get the fancy title of Associate Professor, which

basically means I have to do a whole lot of paperwork for the university as well as juggle tutorials in amongst my regular clinical work. Some days I don't even have time to think. My folks are always at me to slow down, but it's hard to get a good balance of work and play.'

'I know. It's hard when your skills are needed so much.'

'Like you, right?' he guessed.

She lowered her gaze self-consciously. 'I don't have the demands on me that you do.'

'I don't know about that,' he said. 'From what I hear you don't get to play too often either.'

'No, not much, I guess.'

'Are you planning to spend the rest of your life on Niroli?' he asked after a tiny, almost imperceptible pause.

'I'm not sure…' She picked up her glass and stared at its contents. 'I would like to travel, perhaps see a bit of the world, but I have responsibilities here for now.'

'Your father and brothers?'

'Yes…it might be different when my father…passes, but for now I have no immediate plans to leave.'

A small silence settled in the space between them. Amelia was hunting her brain for something to say to break it, when a man suddenly approached their table to stare at Alex, his face almost white with shock. 'Antonio?'

Alex turned his head. 'Sorry, I think you've got the wrong guy.'

'I am sorry…' The man backed away. 'You look like someone I once knew.'

Alex gave him a friendly smile. 'It happens all the time,' he said. 'I guess I have one of those boring generic faces.'

Amelia saw the up and down movement of the other man's throat, his pallor still sickly white. He apologised once more and returned to his table where the two other people sharing a meal with him had their gazes still trained on Alex. Their heads came together as the man resumed his seat, their voices low but extremely agitated if the gesticulations of their hands were any indication.

'Sorry about that.' Alex smiled at her. 'That's the third time that's happened to me this week. One guy even asked if he could take a photo of me. Kind of freaky, huh?'

Amelia stared at him, her heart feeling like a pendulum that had been knocked out of its steady rhythm. 'It's happened before?' She leaned forward in her chair, her voice lowering. 'Here? On…on the island?'

'Yeah, but I guess it's because I look like a native,' he said with a rueful grin. 'I mean, it's not like I can hide it in spite of my Aussie accent. So far I've been mistaken for an Antonio and a Marco. I think there was one other name but I can't remember what it was. Perhaps I look like an Italian movie star—what do you reckon?'

Her heart gave another hard ram against her sternum.

'So…' she paused for a moment to moisten her suddenly bone-dry lips '…you are of Italian heritage?'

'It's on my birth certificate. I was born in Agrigento in Sicily.'

'Sicily?'

'Yes. That's why I thought I'd take up this offer to visit Niroli, being so close and all.'

Amelia stared at the table for a moment as her heart gradually went back to normal.

He had been born in Sicily.

It was on his birth certificate.

He couldn't possibly be…

'I haven't gone there yet but I thought I might,' he said into the silence.

She looked up at him blankly. 'Where?'

'Agrigento.'

'Why?'

'I just thought I'd have a look around. I haven't told my

parents of my plans, but I kind of figured it wouldn't hurt to have a wander around the churchyards, see if I recognise any names.'

'Do you know your original Italian name?'

'Yes. It's a bit of a mouthful—Santocanale.'

'It's…nice… Very Sicilian…'

'It's not bad, I suppose, but of course it went once I was formally adopted. However, I absolutely refused to go by my Italian first name. I changed it as soon as I went to school,' he said with a wry twist to his mouth.

'What is your first name?'

'Alessandro,' he said, sending another shock wave through her chest. 'Mind you, it's kind of different now—most Australians have no trouble with pronouncing unusual names, but thirty-odd years ago I would have been asking to be singled out and bullied for having such an Italian-sounding name. I've been Alex ever since.'

Alex—*Alessandro*…

Amelia's mind was racing along with her heart. People had stopped him in the street, telling him he looked like someone called Antonio…

Antonio Fierezza, the king's son who had been killed two years ago in a yachting accident.

And Marco…

Her heart gave another sudden sickening lurch.

Marco Fierezza, the twin grandson of the king, Antonio's son, the man who had recently given up his right to the Niroli throne to marry the woman he loved more than the kingdom.

The *non*-identical male twin…

'Is something wrong?' Alex leaned forward. 'You've gone a little pale.'

'I'm fine…it's just a bit hot in here…'

'Want to go for a walk along the shore to cool off?' he suggested, offering her a hand as he stood up.

Amelia placed her hand in his, her stomach feeling hollow

and uneasy as he led her past the table of diners who were still watching him with wide, fearful eyes.

The cooler air outside helped to clear the clutter of her mind.

It was impossible, she reassured herself as they made their way down to the gently lapping shore.

It was just a coincidence as Signora Gravano had said the other day. Alex looked as if he had been born and bred on the island, but so too did many other Italians who visited from the mainland. The olive skin and dark eyes were so commonplace it was understandable people would mistake him for someone else.

A coincidence.

That was all it was.

It couldn't possibly be anything else....

'Feeling better now?' Alex asked as a salty sea breeze licked at their faces a short time later.

'Much better.' She tried a smile but it wasn't entirely successful.

'I guess I should take you home and let you get a good night's sleep,' he said, looking down at her, his expression still soft with concern.

'I guess so.'

'Can we do this again?' His deep velvet voice was a brush-like caress against her face.

She ran her tongue across her lips and lowered her eyes. 'You don't have much time here.'

He nudged up her chin with his finger. 'For you I will make the time.'

Amelia looked into his eyes, her chest filling with unexpected emotion. She didn't want to fall in love, certainly not with a man who was only here for a month. How could she bear it when he left if she let her guard down in such a way? But something about Alex Hunter was totally captivating. Not just his sense of humour but also his sincerity. He laughed at life but he also treated it with a great deal of respect. She couldn't help admiring that quality in him. There was a solid depth to his character that no amount of playful banter could hide. His consideration of his adoptive parents' feelings showed his ability to put others' needs before his own, so too did his commitment to the Free Hospital, offering his services free of charge.

It would be all too easy to fall in love with him but where would that leave her in the end?

'Alex…can I ask you a question?' She looked up at him, her hazel gaze troubled.

'Sure.'

'You said that you weren't really interested in finding out who your biological parents were…but what if *they* came looking for you?'

He compressed his lips for a moment as he gave it some thought. 'I don't know…I hadn't thought of it from that angle. I'd always assumed since I was given away at the age of two that my parent—or parents as the case may be—had no further interest in me. How could they? If they had developed a loving relationship with me over that time why would they have had me adopted out?'

It was a salient point, she had to admit. It would be hard enough relinquishing a newborn infant, let alone one you had reared to the age of two, watching all those tiny milestones on the way past. The first smile, the first steps, the first words. How could anyone do it without a very good reason?

'Were you adopted from Sicily or Australia?' she asked.

'Australia,' he said. 'I guess my biological parent or parents had migrated there.'

'What about your sister?' she asked. 'Has she traced her biological parents?'

'Megan was adopted by my parents when she was twelve,'

he said in a sober tone. 'Her biological parents were abusive. I don't think she would ever consider seeing either of them again.'

'How tragic. It must be very hard for her.'

'My parents have done the very best they can to help her overcome her past, but some things are not so easily resolved.'

'I can see why you are so hesitant to go looking for your own birth parents. Like you said, you never know what you might find.'

'Exactly,' he said. 'There are some things in life that are best left well alone.'

She fell into step beside him as they made their way back to his car. Alex Hunter was right, she thought as they drove back towards the turn-off to the foothills.

Some things were better left well alone...

CHAPTER SEVEN

THE cottage was in total darkness when Alex drove up the pot-holed driveway. He glanced at the little figure sitting so silently beside him, wondering if she was going to baulk at going out with him again. He had enjoyed the evening much more than he'd expected to. He knew he had limited time on the island, but it didn't mean he couldn't have a little dalliance without strings. Certainly Amelia Vialli was nothing like any other woman he had ever dated, and after his most recent break-up that was exactly what he needed right now. It had nothing to do with Amelia's lack of experience of the world, although he would be lying to himself if he didn't admit to how quaint and refreshing he found it. So many women he knew were way too polished and worldly, and Sarah, his ex-girlfriend, had been no exception. It was such a change to be in the company of a young woman who didn't hide behind layers of make-up and cloying perfume and flirtatious, manipulative wiles. Amelia had a feisty spirit underneath that quiet humility and he loved that she showed it without reserve. And she was passionate, much more so than he could ever have imagined. One kiss had shown him what was simmering under the surface, no doubt hidden for all this time for fear of being hurt again.

'Would you like me to wait with you until your father and brothers return?' he offered as he brought the car to a standstill.

'No, I'll be fine. They could be ages and you have to operate tomorrow,' she said. 'Thank you for a lovely evening. The meal was wonderful.'

He came around to help her out of the car, the moonlight highlighting the perfect oval of her small pixie face. 'But we didn't even have dessert.' He gave her a twinkling look. 'That's my favourite part of the meal.'

He heard the soft intake of her breath. 'Maybe some other time…'

He smiled as he pressed a soft kiss to the corner of her mouth. 'I'll hold you to that.'

He walked her to the door, waiting for her to light a candle before he left. The soft, flickering light gave her an almost ethereal look as she turned to face him.

'I suppose you're wondering why we don't have electricity connected,' she said, a tiny glimmer of pride showing in her hazel eyes.

'I hadn't noticed,' he lied.

He felt his stomach tighten with anger at how she and her family had been treated. 'It's not right you have to live like this, Amelia. There must be something that can be done. I could speak to someone about it for you.'

She lifted her chin as she held the door open for him. 'We come from completely different worlds, Alex. Don't go looking for a bridge between them. There isn't one.'

'That's crazy and you know it. We are just two ordinary people who are interested in each other. Why not explore that interest and see where it takes us?'

'It will take you back to Australia and leave me here.'

He frowned at her. 'You don't know that.'

'It won't work, Alex. I know it won't.'

'So you're suddenly an expert on intimate relationships after one bad experience in eleven years?' He hadn't meant to sound so angry, but the determination in her manner and tone had got under his normally unflappable skin. 'Come on, Amelia. Give this a chance. We struck sparks off each other from the word go. I haven't felt like that before. I know this could work for now.'

'Do they have a playboy manual that all you men consult to give you the best pick-up lines to use?' she asked with a little curl of her lip. 'So far this evening on at least two occasions you've used the very same lines my ex-lover used to get me to sleep with him.'

Now he *was* really angry. 'Amelia, don't cast me in the same mould as that idiot. I don't see why we can't just see what happens.'

'You want a relationship with an outcast peasant?' she asked with an arch of one brow.

'You are *not* a peasant. I don't see you as anything other than a beautiful young woman who is throwing her life away.'

'So you fancy yourself as Prince Charming intent on rescuing Cinderella from her life of drudgery, do you?' she asked with biting sarcasm.

'I'm no prince,' he said tightly. 'I'm just a regular guy who is very attracted to a woman for the first time in I don't know how long.'

She rolled her eyes. 'That is *such* a line.'

He clenched his fists, trying to get control. 'Look, I can't help it if some things I say have been said before in another context. That's not my problem—that's yours. All I know is I have a short time here and I don't want to waste any of it on arguing when we could be developing a connection instead.'

She gave him a smile touched with sadness. 'You're wasting your time with me, Alex. Go and find yourself someone who is able to move with grace and ease in your world. I would only embarrass you. After all, isn't that really why you bought me this dress? So you could take me out in public without cringing?'

He raked a hand through his hair in frustration. 'I give up. All right, you win. I'll leave you alone. I get the message loud and clear. Sorry it's taken me so long. I must have dating dyslexia or something. You can live your little nun's life hidden up here in the woods—see if I care. I have better things to do with my time than try and get you to change your mind.' He moved through the open door to the moonlight outside. 'I guess I'll see you some time on the ward.'

She didn't answer.

But in a way that was in itself an answer, Alex thought as he drove back down the road, bumping over the pot-holes without a thought to his hire car's suspension.

Amelia Vialli had given him the brush-off and he'd damn well better get over it.

When she came out into the kitchen the next morning Amelia found her father sitting at the table, his pain-glazed eyes briefly meeting hers.

'I do not want anything to eat,' he said as she reached for the utensils to prepare his breakfast.

'But, *Papà*, you have to have something,' she insisted.

He sent her an embittered glance. 'What need does a dying man have for food?'

'*Papà*—' she began.

'Do not patronise me, Amelia.' He gave a hacking cough and continued, 'I know I am dying. As far as I am concerned the sooner it happens, the better.'

'You can't mean that!'

'I do,' he said with a grim look. 'Especially now.'

She frowned at his tone. 'Why…especially now?'

He shifted his eyes from hers and she saw his throat tighten, along with his hands, which were in white-knuckled knots on the table in front of him.

'*Papà?*'

He raised his head to look at her. 'A long time ago...before you and Rico and Silvio were born I did a very bad thing.'

Amelia felt something thick and immovable settle in the middle of her chest, robbing her of the air she needed to breathe. 'W-what sort of bad thing?' she asked, her voice coming out as a cracked whisper.

His eyes were filled with shame as they held hers. 'I was responsible for the kidnap of Prince Alessandro Fierezza.'

She stared at him, her insides shuddering, her heart racing and her palms damp with the dew of dread.

'I am sorry, Amelia,' he went on brokenly. 'I know it is a terrible shock but I was young and got caught up in the rebellion.'

'But you said you were never part of it! You've always told us you were not involved in any way!'

He coughed so hard and for so long, she became seriously frightened. *'Papà?'* She stepped towards him. 'Are you all right?'

He waved his hand as he used the other to bring an old rag to his mouth to spit out the bloody mucus. His gaze returned to hers. 'I started out on the fringe and was never too heavily involved—always kept in the dark. But gradually, over time, I was given more and more responsibility, especially as the movement to kidnap the prince gathered momentum.'

'Y-you...you mean you...*killed* him?'

He shook his head and sighed. 'No, I did not kill him. Do you really believe me capable of such a thing, your own father?'

Amelia swallowed and reached for his age-ridden hand. 'No, *Papà*, but, w-what did you do with him?'

His eyes glistened with moisture, something she had never seen in them before, not even after her mother had died.

'I organised for him to be shipped away,' he said. 'I had some connections, a couple who were prepared to take the child.'

'Take him where?'

'To somewhere he could not be easily traced.'

'But what about the other child?' she asked after a throbbing silence that seemed to be keeping erratic time with her heart. 'The child who is now buried at the palace?'

'King Giorgio had activated an undercover operation to get his grandson back but it backfired. The parents of the child were part of the resistance group and when the explosions happened during the rescue operation they were all killed. Because they had no other relatives it was easy for me to pass the boy off as the prince. No one questioned it. I saw the chance to get out of the contract that had been handed to me.'

'The contract?'

'To kill the prince if the ransom bid failed.'

Amelia stiffened at her father's harsh words. 'But you couldn't go through with it?'

'No.' He gave a ragged sigh. 'He was a little boy of two, barely speaking, crying for his *mamma* and brother all the time. It nearly broke my heart. I just couldn't do it.'

Tears burned at the back of Amelia's eyes. 'Oh, *Papà*.'

'I had to rely on the silence of other people to ship the boy out of danger. It cost me everything. That is why we have lived in poverty ever since. But it was the only thing I could do, Amelia. I suddenly found myself in over my head with the rebellion. Your mother had just found out she was pregnant. I could not extricate myself without losing my life or hers if it became known I had not carried out the plan to kill the prince.'

'Have you heard anything of what happened to him?' she asked.

'There are rumours…' he paused, his throat moving up and down again '…rumours that he is alive and currently on the island.'

Amelia stared at him in growing alarm.

'Of course, no one has verified it but it should not be hard to do so,' he said. 'One look will be enough for me to know if he is the prince.'

'One look?' She frowned at him in bafflement. 'But, *Papà*, a tiny child of two will be hard to recognise thirty-four years later, surely?'

His pain-filled eyes came back to hers. 'Prince Alessandro has a birthmark, a strawberry one. I saw it when I was looking after him. It is very distinctive. It is shaped like the island of Niroli.'

'A birthmark…' she breathed. 'Where?'

'It is on his right forearm, on the underside near the elbow. You would not see it unless he turned his arm right over.'

Amelia let out her breath in a jagged stream, her thoughts clanging together in her head like discordant cathedral bells. She mentally backtracked, going over each time she had been with Alex Hunter, trying to recall whether he had been wearing shirt sleeves or whether they had been rolled up….

'The new doctor,' her father said into the heavy silence. 'I want to see him. But it must be in private. Up here. Can you arrange it?'

'Why him, *Papà*?'

'I want to make sure.'

She swallowed again. 'Y-you think Dr Hunter is the prince?'

'I do not know but I must make certain before I die.'

The stark reality of the situation was fast dawning on Amelia and it terrified her. If news got out of her father's role in the kidnap of the prince he would be hauled before the courts and charged. His last few weeks of life would be spent in prison, not with his family. Their name would again be vilified in every way imaginable; her brothers would never find work again on the island and her life would be even more difficult than it currently was.

And if it was true that Alex Hunter was indeed Prince Alessandro, what would that information do to him? How would he cope with the news that he was not a simple commoner but a member of the richest royal family in Europe? And not only a member, with his twin brother's recent decision—now the rightful heir to the throne…

Her father jolted her out of her tortured reverie. 'I want you to know that I am prepared to be punished for what I did, Amelia. I have always been prepared, but I did not come forward at the time for your mother's sake. I kept everything from her. I had to. She was expecting a child, your brother Rico. I did not want her to see me as a man capable of such a crime. It was even worse after your brothers and you were born. Having my own children made me realise the enormity of what I had done. I could tell no one and the fight to keep those who knew silent became all the more desperate. It has cost me dearly.'

'It has cost the prince his birthright!' she said, unable to contain her despair and shame at what he had done. 'No matter if the Australian doctor is the prince or not, whoever the prince is now has been robbed of everything that is rightly his. He has never known his real parents, never lived on the island, and never spoken the language and a thousand other things that can never be replaced or put right by a last-minute deathbed confession!'

'I know, but I must put right what I can,' he said. 'I must see this man who has the whole island talking of his likeness to Antonio Fierezza.'

'And Prince Marco,' she put in heavily.

'Is that true?' he asked, his throat moving up and down again. 'You have seen Prince Marco up at the palace, have you not? Does he look anything like the doctor?'

She frowned as she thought about it. There was a similarity; they were both dark of hair and eyes, although she seemed to recall Marco's were not as coal-black as Alex's, and he seemed a bit taller, not much, maybe only an inch if that.

'I don't know…maybe a little bit,' she said.

'So you will do this for me? Bring the doctor to me as soon as you can arrange it?'

'He was here last night,' she informed him.

He coughed out the word. *'Here?'*

She nodded. 'He came across me on the road. and gave me a lift and somehow talked me into having dinner with him. I decided to go because you and Silvio were out. Where is Silvio, by the way?'

'He has been working on a boat that goes between here and Sicily. He heard the rumours and took me down to the port to talk to some people who had seen the doctor and become suspicious.'

'*Papà*…you do realise if Alex Hunter is the child you spirited away that there will be consequences, not just for you, but for Rico and Silvio and me?'

'Yes…' His thin chest deflated on a ragged breath. 'I have thought long and hard about it. For some years now, in spite of my efforts to distance myself from the organisation, my name has been brought up whenever the Vialli bandits are mentioned. Every finger is now pointing to me. I cannot allow you or your brothers to live any longer under the shame of a murder that never took place.'

'The kidnap of a small child is almost as bad.'

'I did the best I could do under the circumstances,' he said. 'I did not kill him. I had every chance but I did not do it. I would like to tell that to him…to ask for forgiveness. Then I can die in peace.'

She let out another sigh. 'There can be no peace, *Papà*, can't you see that? Not now, not if what you've said is true.'

'What would you have me do?' he asked. 'If he is the prince, he has the right to know.'

'But what if he's not?'

Her father looked at her, the sadness of his life shining in his eyes. 'Just bring him to me, Amelia. Bring the Australian doctor to me so I can find out once and for all.'

CHAPTER EIGHT

'AREN'T you heading up to Theatre to watch the procedure?' Lucia asked when Amelia came on the ward the next morning.

'I thought I would give it a miss,' she answered, putting her bag in the bottom drawer of the filing cabinet in the nurses' station and turning the key.

She had spent a sleepless night thinking about her father's confession, her mind unable to grasp the enormity of what he had done. The thought of trying to remain professionally calm watching Alex Hunter perform a highly technical procedure while suspecting what she did was unthinkable.

'But Dr Morani organised cover for you down here on the ward,' Lucia said. 'He wants you in particular to see how Dr Hunter performs the off-pump procedure.'

'I'm sure I'll hear all about it.'

'Hearing is one thing, seeing is another,' Lucia said. 'If I were you I'd go. There's not much happening here. I might even get time for a cup of coffee if Signor Ruggio in bed eight behaves himself.'

Amelia forced a little smile to her lips at the mention of their elderly patient. 'He's such a sweet old man and never complains.'

'He's a cheeky old flirt, that's what he is. But you're

right—he's a sweet man.' Lucia gave her a probing look. 'Is something wrong? You look worried. Is it your father again?'

'Yes…' At least that wasn't a lie, Amelia thought. 'But it's nothing I can't deal with.'

'Well, if there's anything I can do just let me know,' Lucia offered. 'Oh, here's the nurse who's covering for you.'

'They're waiting for you in Theatre,' the fill-in nurse said.

Amelia tried to disguise her panic but Lucia wasn't fooled. She gave her a little grin. 'You're not going to go all squeamish now, are you?'

'Of course not,' Amelia said with already sagging confidence. 'I've been to Theatre enough times to know it's not always a pretty sight.'

'Just as well the visiting surgeon is so easy on the eye,' Lucia said. 'If you can't bear looking at the patient, look at him instead.'

I will be looking at him, Amelia wanted to say. *Very closely.*

Amelia made her way to the change room and changed into Theatre gear. The operating staff were busily preparing when she arrived in the cardiac theatre.

The patient, a man in his early fifties with a long family history of heart disease, had already been anaesthetised. He wasn't attached to the bypass pump although it was available and primed if an emergency situation developed.

'Stand in here near the anaesthetic machine, Sister,' directed the anaesthetist. 'I can stay out of your way so you can get a good look at the procedure.'

As she moved into position Alex Hunter emerged from the scrub room, arms in the air ready for the scout nurse to assist with gowning. It was a perfect opportunity for Amelia to see his uncovered arms, but just as she moved to gain a better look the instrument nurse moved in front of her with a tray and blocked her view.

Alex turned around once he was gowned and gloved and met her eyes. 'How nice you could join us, Sister Vialli. I take it you had no other pressing engagements?'

So he was still annoyed with her for rejecting him, Amelia mused as she lifted her chin. 'I am here, as you see,' she said.

He held her defiant look for a moment before turning to the anaesthetist. 'Carlo, you can start the heparin now, one milligram per kilo heparin, and we'll monitor the clotting profile every half-hour as we go through in the protocol.'

'Right,' Carlo said, beginning the IV heparin infusion.

Amelia watched from the head of the operating table as the patient was prepped and draped by Alex together with the cardiac registrar and the scrub nurse.

Alex made a midline incision over the sternum, and, using the powered bone saw, completed a median sternotomy, his deep, calm voice taking the theatre staff through each step. As Alex and the registrar opened the chest, Dr Morani harvested the left long-saphenous vein in the patient's left leg to be used for the bypass.

Alex then took the team step by step through the moving-heart bypass procedure, taking special care to show how the vessel stabiliser was used to reduce movement of the vessels to be sutured during the movement of the heart.

'As you can see, Dr Morani, the vessel stabiliser must be adjusted so as not to leave too much coronary artery exposed, otherwise movement is not damped enough, and getting a good quality anastomosis becomes a real struggle,' Alex explained.

'Yes, that appears the hardest bit to get right,' the surgeon agreed. 'That's much clearer now—even I could do the anastomosis now that you've set it up.'

'I'm sure you could do as good a job as me, Doctor, but I'd like to do the first anastomosis to show you a couple of tricks to damp down movements between the instruments and the heart.' He flicked a glance from above his surgical mask in the direction of Amelia. 'What do you think of the procedure so far, Sister Vialli?'

'You are obviously well practised in working with the heart,' she answered.

'You have to have an intuitive feel for the heart in this type of surgery,' he said, then, addressing the senior cardiac surgeon beside him, added, 'Now it's your turn, Dr Morani. We'll set up the vessel dampening clamps for the LAD and you can do the second anastomosis.'

Under Alex's guidance, the fellow surgeon sutured the freed-up internal mammary artery to the LAD distal to its stenosis. Finally, using the Doppler flow meter, Alex was happy that blood flow into the bypassed coronaries was satisfactory and left the senior surgeon and the registrar to routinely close the chest.

As Alex stripped off his gloves and gown he turned from the laundry bin to see Amelia staring at him, and folded his arms across his chest, his dark eyes narrowing and hardening as they met hers. 'Are you by any chance waiting to speak to me, Sister?'

'No…no, I was just leaving.'

'Don't let me keep you. I'm sure you have plenty of things to do on the ward.'

She wanted to stare him down, but in the end she had to push her pride to one side. 'Actually I would like to speak to you if I may.'

'I'll have to check my diary to see if I can squeeze you in.'

'I would appreciate it…thank you.'

'Dr Hunter, there's a phone call on line one for you,' one of the scout nurses informed him. 'It's a young woman. She wouldn't give me her name.'

Amelia saw the flicker of something in his dark eyes before he turned away to address the nurse. 'Can you put it through to the office next door?' he asked.

By the time he turned back to Amelia she had a cynical set to her mouth. 'It hasn't taken you long to find a replacement, has it?' she said in an undertone.

'Last time I checked I was a free man,' he returned coolly. 'Now, if you'll excuse me I'd better take that call.'

Amelia watched as he shouldered open the theatre change-room door, his arms now stiffly by his sides…

'There's a message for you, Amelia,' Lucia informed her as soon as she returned from her afternoon tea break later that day. 'Signora Gravano wants you to call on her this afternoon after your shift finishes, as if you haven't got enough to do.'

'It's all right,' Amelia said, wondering if the old woman had had another fall and reopened her leg wound. 'She's lonely with her daughter living abroad. I'll go straight there after I finish.'

Once her shift was over Amelia left a message for Rico at the front desk in case he arrived to pick her up before she got back, and made her way to the old lady's house.

There was no sign of movement at Alex's cottage although it appeared as if he or someone had done some preliminary work in the garden. The brambles had been trimmed back and the sweet smell of newly cut grass filled her nostrils on the way past.

Signora Gravano didn't really need her leg redressing but seemed in want of a chat, so Amelia sat with her for a while, all the time trying not to glance at the clock on the wall. Rico wasn't the most patient of young men and she knew if she didn't come out on time he would leave without her. There was a bus that took her as far as the turn-off to the cottage, but that still meant a walk of at least five kilometres.

'I have heard some disturbing rumours I think you should be informed of if you haven't already heard them,' Signora Gravano said just as Amelia finally made a move to leave.

'Oh?' she said, wondering why the old woman had waited

until now to state the real reason for her request to see her. 'What rumours are they?'

'People are saying that Prince Alessandro is not dead after all,' Signora Gravano informed her.

Amelia hoped her face wasn't showing the panic and dread she was feeling. 'That seems rather far-fetched,' she said. 'I mean, the child's grave is at the palace for anyone to see.'

'I know, but there could be another explanation for that— some other child put in his place, for instance.'

'I suppose that's a possibility, but you know what these rumours are like. They come and go and are best ignored,' Amelia said.

'I have heard the king's medical advisors noticed a startling similarity to Antonio Fierezza when they were researching the new technique Dr Hunter is pioneering. Dr Hunter's photograph was in the medical journal they had researched and they began to wonder if he was in some way related to the family.'

Amelia sat back down, not because she wanted to but because her legs were threatening to give way. 'Is that why he received a royal summons?' she asked.

'It makes sense, does it not?' the old woman said. 'The king does need heart surgery, of course, but this was a way of bringing Dr Hunter to Niroli to see if the likeness was something that needed further investigation by the royal officials.'

'It is said we all have a double somewhere in the world,' Amelia said, trying to put some rationality in place. 'It's just one of those things.'

'Perhaps, but if what they suspect is true, there will be hell to pay.'

Amelia moistened her dry-as-dust mouth. 'You mean for whomever is responsible?'

'I would not like to be that person,' Signora Gravano said, her black eyes suddenly very direct. 'They have been responsible for a terrible crime for which they have never been charged.'

Amelia forced her shoulders to relax. 'It is surely a better outcome than the original verdict of murder…I mean, if the prince is in fact still alive…somewhere…'

'Yes, indeed, but how will the prince feel once he finds out his true identity? His biological parents are dead. He will never have the chance to meet them in person. And what of Prince Marco, who for all this time has grieved the loss of his twin?'

'I am sure the prince can't even remember his twin brother,' Amelia said, recalling her conversation with Alex. 'He was far too young.'

The old woman grunted. 'He has lived with his parents' grief, which would have no doubt affected him and his sisters.'

'Is Alex Hunter aware of any of this…er…speculation?'

'I am not sure. He is going to the palace this evening to meet the king. Perhaps the subject will be raised then,' Signora Gravano said.

'Someone should prepare him…' Amelia got to her feet, testing her legs, which still felt watery. 'It would be unfair to surprise him with this information without some sort of lead up.'

Signora Gravano smiled sagely. 'That is why I asked you to come, Amelia. You will understand much better than the palace staff about the sensitive nature of this. Dr Hunter should be home by now. Why not go around and talk to him now before he leaves for his meeting with the king?'

Amelia ignored the short cut and made her way past Alex's hire car to his front door, her hand visibly shaking as she lifted it to the brass knocker.

There was no answer.

She frowned as she looked back at the car parked in the shade. He must be somewhere about. He had finished at the hospital at least two hours ago.

'Are you looking for me?' Alex asked from the other side of the front step.

She swung around to face him, her throat closing up at the sight of him dressed in running shorts and T-shirt, the perspiration from his workout plastering the material to his toned body. 'Er…yes…' she said. 'I was hoping to catch you before you left for the palace.'

One of his dark brows rose in an arc above his right eye. 'Why?'

She shifted from foot to foot. 'I wanted to speak to you—privately.'

Alex held her anxious gaze for a lengthy moment. She looked tired and he felt a little ashamed of his attitude earlier. He blew out a breath and motioned for her to go inside. 'Come on, I've got something I need to say to you too.'

He waited until she was seated and with a cold drink in front of her before he took the chair opposite, giving his face a quick rub with a hand towel. 'So who's going to go first?' he asked.

'I don't mind.' She chewed her bottom lip momentarily and added, 'You can if you like.'

'Right,' he said as he pushed the towel to one side. 'I have an apology to make. I was an idiot last night. Simple as that. No wonder you gave me the heave-o.' He sent his fingers through the damp thickness of his hair, a small frown beetling his brows. 'I don't know why I came on so strong,' he continued. 'I know you're not going to believe this, but it's really not my style at all.' He gave her a sheepish look and added, 'I guess it's been too long between relationships or something.'

She twisted her mouth wryly. 'I bet it wasn't as long as eleven years.'

'No.' He laughed lightly. 'More like eleven months, but long enough to make me a bit trigger-happy.'

'It's all right. I understand.'

'I wish you did.'

'I do,' she insisted.

'Believe me, you don't.'

'How do you know what I feel?' she asked.

He smiled at her then. 'Yep, that vow of silence would never have worked.'

She started to purse her mouth but thought better of it. 'I didn't come here to argue with you,' she said.

'Where do you usually go?'

'Must you make a joke of everything?' she asked in frustration. 'I'm trying to be serious here.'

'So am I, Amelia.' He reached for the towel once more. 'Now what did you come all this way to tell me?'

Amelia stared at his right arm as he lifted it to his face to wipe the moisture from his brow, her breath coming to a stumbling halt in her chest.

There was absolutely no sign of a birthmark.

CHAPTER NINE

ALEX put the towel back down and caught her staring at him. 'Is something wrong?'

'No…no, nothing.' Amelia lowered her gaze and focussed on the table separating them. She'd checked his left arm while he'd changed hands to dry off, but it too was clear of any distinctive birthmarks.

'What did you come here to tell me?' he asked into the suddenly crackling silence.

'It was nothing important.' She got to her feet and pushed in the chair. 'I should get going. The last bus leaves at six-thirty.'

'Wait.' He came around to her side and stalled her with a hand on her arm. 'Listen, I know this is going to sound really dumb, but would you consider doing me a favour tonight?'

Amelia met his dark gaze, her heart and stomach still both feeling as if they had just performed a complicated gymnastics routine. 'W-what is it?'

His hand fell away from her arm, his expression turning awkward again. 'To tell you the truth I'm a bit nervous about going to the palace tonight. I know it's a lot to ask, but, since you go there all the time, would you consider coming with me tonight sort of as moral support?'

She stared at him for a beat or two, wondering if he was

genuine or whether this was another ploy to get her to go out with him. 'I don't go there *all* the time,' she corrected him.

'But at least you've met the king and the staff and are more or less familiar with the layout of the place.'

'If you think I believe for even one second that you are intimidated in any way by royalty, you must think me even more gullible than I thought,' she said. 'Besides, the royal aides will escort you in and escort you out. Don't worry—you won't get lost and end up in a dungeon with chains around your ankles.'

'What if I strike up a deal with you?' he said with a little glint in his eyes. 'If you come with me to the palace I will give you a ride home and visit your father, free of charge. Will he be home tonight?'

Five minutes ago Amelia would not have bought in to his offer, but now, with his arm showing no sign of the birthmark that would have sent her father to prison, she knew she would have to accept. Without that sign there was nothing to connect her father to the disappearance of the prince all those years ago. She wanted her father to see it for himself, to put his fears to rest. Besides, her last glance at her watch had told her the bus would have long gone. A taxi fare was out of the question even if she could convince a driver to take his car up the somewhat perilous section of road.

'All right,' she said. 'It's a deal. But I will have to stay in the background. I'm still wearing my uniform.'

'That's OK.' He smiled a victor's smile. 'I'm only going to be there for ten minutes or so according to the invitation I received. I'll just grab a quick shower. Make yourself at home.'

Amelia let out her breath once he had gone to the bathroom and wondered if she should still warn him of the suspicions or leave it for him to deal with if and when they were raised during his visit. No doubt the king would be looking closely for the mark that would establish his lost grandson's identity.

How he would do so she couldn't even hazard a guess. But she reasoned that if, like her, the king saw the clear skin on Alex Hunter's arm he might not even raise the topic at all, simply treating the visit as the royal summons as which it was originally portrayed. The rumours would hopefully die down and she would then be able to nurse her father to his final rest without the threat of exposure.

Alex came out a few minutes later looking refreshed and smelling of his aftershave, a heady combination of lemons and spice that reminded Amelia of the sun-drenched citrus orchards on the island.

She felt grubby and uncomfortable in her uniform, especially now he was dressed in a dark suit and tie, the crisp whiteness of his shirt highlighting the healthy colour of his skin and the darkness of his eyes. He had shaved, which she assumed he would have to do twice a day to keep that chiselled jaw smooth. Her skin gave a little all-over shiver as she thought about how his mouth had felt on hers, and the gentle but imminently sexy abrasion of his skin as it had moved over the creamy softness of her face.

She watched as he straightened his tie, the movement of his neck indicating it probably wasn't his preferred choice of dress.

'Is my tie tucked in at the back?' he asked, turning around for her to inspect it.

She had to stand on tiptoe to tuck a thin strip of his tie under the collar, her fingers skating over his skin as if they had a mind of their own. 'There…that's it,' she said a little breathlessly.

He turned back around before she could step away, his eyes locking with hers. Amelia felt the air between them begin to tighten as if an invisible force were drawing her inexorably closer to him. She could even feel the sway of her body towards him, her chest brushing against his as his hands came out to hold her steady.

His eyes grew darker as his head came closer, the warmth of his mint-flavoured breath caressing her up-tilted face. She felt her eyelids dropping as his mouth came down, the first brush of his lips on hers setting her alight like a match to a meticulously laid fire. The combustion was instantaneous and enthralling; there was nothing she could do to hold back her response. It consumed her totally, the sensations rushing through her like a hot river of flame.

His tongue came searching for hers, drawing it into an intimate tangle of slow but drugging dance-like movements, each intimate thrust mimicking the pulse of his lower body where it was pressed so close to hers. She could feel the imprint of his maleness, the hard evidence of how his body responded to hers. It excited her to think he was still attracted to her, even though she had done her best to spurn him. It showed he wasn't going to go down without a fight, that he would throw everything he could at their developing relationship no matter what the cost.

But any cost would be hers, she hastily reminded herself. As thrilling at this sizzling attraction was, it wasn't going to last beyond a month, not unless he was prepared to take her with him, which seemed an impossible dream. He had a life in Australia, a busy career, a loving family and a chance to change the world with this pioneering breakthrough in cardiac surgery.

What place could she have in such a life? She had been reared in poverty and shame, her life so far spent in the service of others.

And yet what made this attraction all the more irresistible was she was no longer a young naïve girl hardly out of her teens. She was a fully grown woman now, with needs and desires that could no longer be ignored. She had thrown herself into hard work to distract herself from the emptiness of her existence, but now it seemed as if that lonely existence was crying out for more. She wanted to feel like an attractive woman again. She wanted to be swept up in the magic of emotion and desire.

She wanted Alex Hunter even if she could only have him temporarily....

Alex pulled back reluctantly, his breathing still choppy. 'Whoa there, princess,' he said. 'I'm drifting out of my depth here.'

'I'm sorry.'

'Hey,' he said, cupping her face so she couldn't escape his gaze. 'Don't be embarrassed. It's a good thing. In fact it's a rare thing. I don't usually lose my head in these types of situations.'

'I'm sure you're just saying that.'

'I wish I was, truly.' His expression was surprisingly sincere.

'I don't know what to say....' She lowered her gaze, her tongue running over her lips, tasting him, savouring him.

'Don't say anything,' he said. 'Let's just take it one step at a time.'

She raised her eyes back to his. 'I'm frightened, Alex. I don't want to let things get out of control.'

He let out a sigh and hugged her close. 'I know you're frightened, but you don't need to be. I want you and I intend to have you. Surely you know that by now?'

She leaned back to look up at him, her stomach quivering at the determined promise of his statement. 'Is that why you've been so persistent?'

'Have I been persistent?'

She gave him a mock-reproving look, desperately trying to maintain a level head when all she wanted to do was throw herself back into his arms. 'You know you have,' she said. 'You just won't take no for an answer.'

'Well, can you blame me? As soon as I met you I felt something drop into place, as if a piece of a puzzle had been missing all this time and now I'd suddenly found it.'

She narrowed her eyes at him. 'So who was the woman who phoned you today?'

'It was my sister, Megan. She's backpacking around Europe and wanted to say hi.'

It was impossible to disguise her tiny sigh of relief. 'She's lucky to have a brother like you,' she said.

'That's what I keep telling her, but do you think she will listen?' His smile lit up his eyes.

'I like you, Alex Hunter,' she said softly. 'I really like you.'

'That's a start, I guess,' he said, his dark eyes twinkling. 'Any chance of an upgrade on that?'

She met his smile with one of her own. 'Perhaps. I'll have to think about it.'

'Well, in the meantime I'll try and be patient,' he said and brought his mouth back down to hers.

This time his kiss was even more demanding, the searing thrust of his tongue taking her breath away as his hands skimmed her curves. Her breasts leapt at his touch, even though the fabric of her uniform still covered them. She could feel herself being swept away on the tide of spiralling need that flowed between them. She could feel it in his body, the energy and strength that pulsed there. She could taste it in his kiss, the heat and fire that burned against her mouth as she returned his kiss with fevered urgency. She could feel it in her own body, the ache and throb of unmet needs that refused to be denied any longer.

'This is crazy,' Alex said, suddenly pulling away. 'My timing as usual is way off. I have to be at the palace in ten minutes. That's not nearly long enough to pleasure you in the way I want to.'

Amelia felt her stomach hollow at his words. 'We can do this some other time,' she said, surprising herself more than him. 'That's if you still want to….'

He pressed a quick, hard kiss to her mouth. 'I want to. I'll be thinking of nothing else the whole time I'm with the king.'

She wrinkled her nose at him. 'I'm sure he would be very shocked to hear that.'

He smiled down at her. 'I don't care if he is. What's an old man with a medieval castle got to do with me? I'd much rather be with you.'

Amelia decided then to tell him of the rumours. What harm could it do for him to know? At least then he would be able to meet the king's questions levelly now there was no doubt he was not the prince.

'Alex…there's something you should know before you meet the king… Something important.'

Alex frowned at her grave tone. 'What?'

She took a steadying breath. 'You're probably going to think this is ridiculous in the extreme, but there have been rumours circulating on the island ever since you arrived that you are in some way related to the king.'

'Related?' His frown deepened.

'You remember the kidnap and murder of the king's grandson we discussed the other day?'

He gave a brief nod without responding.

'Well,' she said, 'there's been a recent disclosure that the infant prince was not in fact murdered as first thought, but spirited away to be brought up by someone else.'

'Someone else where?' he asked.

'I don't know all the details, just that the prince—according to my sources—was well and truly alive the last time…this person saw him.'

'So what's all this got to do with me?' he asked, his brow still furrowed.

'At the restaurant last night you were mistaken for someone else. You said it had happened ever since you arrived on the island. I thought you should know that the king as well as others has seen a likeness in your features to his dead son,

Antonio, and his surviving grandson, Marco. They've been wondering if you are in fact the prince.'

His breath came out in a whooshing rush. 'Amelia, this island is teeming with male look-alikes. There's hardly a man here who doesn't have black hair and brown eyes.'

'I know… I just thought I should tell you, that's all. It seemed a little far-fetched to me when I first heard, but then when you said you were adopted and that your Italian name was Alessandro I started to wonder about it myself.'

Alex gave a chuckle of incredulous laughter. 'Far-fetched? It's bloody ridiculous! Me? A prince? Don't make me laugh.'

Amelia started to smile. 'I guess it does sound a bit crazy, doesn't it?'

'Just wait till my sister hears about this.' He grinned. 'It's not every day one gets mistaken for royalty. A mate of mine once got mistaken for a famous actor. He even had to sign autographs as the fans just wouldn't believe he wasn't the real deal, but I think this is going one better than that.'

'I hope you didn't mind me telling you,' she said. 'I just thought it would be better to know about it in case they ask you any personal questions at the palace tonight.'

He dropped a quick kiss to the soft bow of her mouth. 'You did the right thing telling me. To tell you the truth I was starting to get a little spooked by all the weird looks I was getting. Now I can rest easy.'

So can I, Amelia thought as they made their way out to his car. *Thank goodness he was plain old Alex Hunter and not the missing prince....*

The fourteenth-century castle was situated on a rocky promontory overlooking the main port of Niroli, the hills behind covered with scented orange groves.

Amelia looked up at it standing so majestically over all it surveyed. The palace had its own private beach and boat houses and the views over the wide horizons were breathtaking. As settings went it was surely one of the most spectacular in the region if not the entire world.

'Quite some beach house,' Alex remarked from beside her.

She smiled and took a step backwards as the royal officials approached. 'I'll wait for you over there,' she said, pointing to a sun-drenched terrace where a bougainvillea vine was trailing over the balustrade in a scarlet arras.

Alex gave her a wink and made his way towards the castle entrance flanked on either side by the uniformed officials.

Amelia turned to look at the sea sparkling in the distance, the tang of salt reaching her from below.

She turned about twenty minutes later as she heard the sound of footsteps and watched as Alex walked towards her, a hint of a smile reflected in his dark eyes as they met hers.

'How was it?' she asked once they were back in his car.

'As house calls go it was certainly unusual,' he said. 'I met with the king and discussed his treatment options. I spoke to him of the risks involved with a patient his age and how I would be prepared to do it at the private hospital as a one-off in a couple of days.'

'Did he mention anything to you about the rumours?'

'No and I didn't bring the topic up. I thought someone was going to at one stage. I was getting some pretty intense scrutiny from the staff as they served drinks, but apart from a few questions about my background things were pretty relaxed.'

'Did you meet any of the royal family? Prince Marco or Prince Luca or the princesses?'

'I did, actually,' he said. 'If you hadn't told me what you had, I would have thought it a bit unusual since I was ostensibly there to see the king on a health matter, but I guess they too wanted to check on any likeness. They were very polite and seemed interested in the procedure I'm pioneering, but they didn't stay long.'

'Could you see any likeness to yourself?' she asked.

'Not so much with Prince Marco or Prince Luca, although of course there are similarities, but I did happen to see a portrait of Antonio and his wife Francesca on one of the walls as I walked past.'

Amelia glanced at him. 'And?'

His eyes met hers briefly, a small frown bringing his brows together as he returned to the task of driving. 'I know this is going to sound a bit strange, but I felt like I'd seen them before. Crazy, huh?'

'Perhaps you've seen a photograph of them in the press,' she suggested. 'The news of their yachting accident hit the headlines all over the world.'

'Yeah, that's probably what it was,' he said, sending her a quick smile.

Amelia settled back in her seat, but the next time she chanced a glance at him his smile had disappeared....

CHAPTER TEN

'How about we have a quick dinner at my place before I visit your father?' Alex suggested a short time later.

'I don't want to put you to any trouble…'

'I'm not quite a celebrity chef or anything, but I can whip up a mean omelette and salad. My mother always told me women are super impressed by a man who can cook.'

'I'm super impressed by a man who can clean up *after* he cooks,' Amelia said with a wry smile. 'My father and brothers are absolutely hopeless.'

'You have it tough up there, don't you?' he asked as he led her into the cottage. 'But you have no need to be ashamed. Home is home, Amelia.'

She lowered her eyes. 'I'm sorry I was so rude to you last night. I'm just not used to people seeing where I live.'

'I've seen some wonderful mansions in my time, and, let me tell you, some miserable souls living in them,' he said. 'Some of the happiest and most well-adjusted people I've met have lived in virtual squalor. Where you live is not important, it's who you are as a person.'

She smiled up at him. 'So while you were up at the palace did you think about how it would be to live like a prince?'

'Yeah, I did a bit, but do you know something? I think it would get on my nerves after a while. All those eyes watching your every move and obsequious staff rushing to pull out your chair for you, or wipe a crumb off your lap. *Sheesh!* I bet you couldn't even go the bathroom without someone peering through the keyhole to see if you really are human after all.'

Amelia laughed. 'I'm sure it's not that bad!'

He grinned as he pulled her towards him. 'What do you say, little elf? Shall we have our main course now or go straight to dessert?'

She gazed up at him with shining eyes. 'What did you have in mind for dessert?'

His mouth came down towards hers, his warm breath caressing the surface of her lips. 'How about strawberry kisses?'

'Is there such a dessert?' she asked breathlessly.

He pressed his mouth against hers for a moment before running his tongue over his lips as if to taste her. 'Yep, there definitely is,' he said, 'and I can't get enough of it.'

Amelia totally melted as his mouth moved over hers, his sensual tongue pushing between her lips to find her own. Each sweeping, sexy movement set her on fire; her skin tingled and shivered with the warm glide of his hands as they moved to shape her form. She felt his hands cup the light weight of her breasts and her stomach hollowed as he began to undo the top buttons of her uniform, one by one, leaving a trail of scorching kisses as he went. Her bra slipped to the floor along with her uniform, leaving her at the mercy of his hungry dark gaze.

'You're so beautiful.' He almost growled the words, so deep and low was his voice as he pulled the tie from his throat and tossed it to the floor.

Her hands helped him with his shirt, her fingers skating over the buttons until it too was at their feet along with her uniform. He stepped out of his trousers and she felt the full thrust of his body against her, the heat of his arousal burning into the soft skin of her stomach.

'Am I going too fast for you?' he said next to her ear where he was nibbling her until her skin started to lift all over.

'Not fast enough,' she breathed and, kicking off her shoes, pushed herself closer.

'It's been a long time for both of us,' he said as he kissed the upper side of one breast. 'I want to pace myself but you're making it hard for me.'

'I can't help it,' she said, and started kissing his throat, hot, sucking little kisses that made him groan with need. 'I want you.'

He picked her up and carried her to his bedroom, his weight coming down on top of her as he joined her, his long legs anchoring her to the bed. He kissed his way down her stomach but she wouldn't let him go below her belly button. She brought his head back up and wriggled until he was pushing against her soft folds.

He wrenched his mouth off hers long enough to gasp something about a condom and she waited impatiently as he reached across her to find one. She heard him rummaging about in the drawer with little success.

'Damn!'

'Here.' She pushed him aside. 'Let me have a girl look.'

'A girl look?'

She smiled coyly as she found a little foil packet and held it up. 'See?'

'I swear you must have planted that in there.'

'I did not! You just weren't looking.'

He ripped the packet open with his teeth and handed her the condom. 'Why don't you put it on in case I can't find what I'm looking for?'

She bit her lip in sudden shyness. 'No…you do it… I might not do it properly.'

He lifted her chin so she met his eyes. 'That's what I like about you, little elf. You're so adorably shy.'

A small frown wrinkled her brow. 'I can't help it.'

He kissed the little crease on her forehead. 'I've never made love to a woman like you before.'

Her brow wrinkled even more. 'Like me?'

He smiled and, taking her hand, placed it on the rigidity of his erection. 'Amelia, do you see what you are doing to me?'

'Oh…'

'You're not disappointed?'

'Why would I be disappointed?' she asked.

'If the rumours were true about me, you could be seconds away from sleeping with a prince. Isn't that every girl's dream?'

Amelia looked at his mouth, the sexy curve of his smile sending sparks of sensation right to the core of her being. 'Just how many seconds are we talking about here?' she asked.

He smiled and pushed her back down, taking her breath away with his first deep thrust, and covered her mouth with his.

The silky slide of his thick body in hers was almost too much for her sensation-starved body to cope with. She felt every nerve jump to attention, every single cell and pore screaming for more and more of his touch. He drove deeper and deeper, obviously trying to pace himself, but she was too greedy for more and lifted her hips to bring him closer. She felt him brush against the pearl of her desire but the tingling sensation didn't last long enough to bring her the release she craved. He shifted position, driving forward with increasing urgency until she was almost screaming with the intimate slippery abrasion of his body rubbing so closely against hers. She arched her back and suddenly everything fell into place. He was where she most wanted him, the deeper, longer strokes of his aroused length taking her to lift-off so that her senses finally soared into oblivion.

She was vaguely aware of his own release, the deep throb of his heart against her naked breasts as he pumped himself into her, his body collapsing like a wind-depleted sail as soon as it was over.

Amelia gently stroked the length of his back, amazed at how she had responded to him but even more amazed at how he had responded to her.

Alex lifted himself up on one elbow to look at her. 'I hope this doesn't sound like a line from that playboy manual you referred to the other night, but that was the most amazing experience I've had in years.'

Amelia ran her hand up and down his forearm in a tickling caress. 'It does sound a bit like something on about page twenty-three, but I agree, it was amazing. Certainly nothing like I've ever experienced before.'

He let out a deep, contented sigh as she moved her fingers farther along his arm. 'That feels nice. You have such soft hands.'

Amelia watched the pathway of her fingers as they went towards his elbow, her brow furrowing when she came to some tiny white, almost undetectable scars on the underside of his arm. 'What did you do to yourself here?' she asked.

He looked down at where she was pointing. 'Oh, that. That was years ago. I had some laser work done.'

'Laser work?' She sat up and stared at him. 'Laser work for what?'

'I had a birthmark.'

She stared at him in shock. 'A birthmark?' she gasped.

He gave her a world-weary look. 'And here I was thinking you were going to be different. That's why I had it removed in the first place.'

'Y-you had it removed?' she croaked.

'My ex-girlfriend Sarah hated it,' he said with a curl of his lip. 'So did a couple of other girlfriends in the past. Quite frankly I couldn't see what the fuss was all about. It was only small and no one could see it unless I had my arm in a certain position.'

You had a birthmark? Amelia was aware she was still gaping at him but there was nothing she could do to stop it. *A strawberry birthmark?*

'Don't worry, Amelia, it's not catching.'

'But…but you don't understand…'

He got off the bed and roughly disposed of the condom. 'Oh, I understand all right. I've been dealing with this for years. What is it with women these days? A birthmark isn't contagious. It's not as if any children I sire will inherit it or anything.'

'Alex—'

'Don't start, Amelia.' He rounded on her. 'I had enough of this from Sarah.'

Amelia knew she was still staring at him but she couldn't seem to get her voice to work.

'Ever heard of a copper bromide machine?' he asked. 'Or perhaps the newer V-beam machine used in laser and sclerotherapy clinics?'

Her eyes widened, her heart starting to hammer in her chest. 'You mean for the…the removal of lesions?'

'Lesions, pigmentation, spider veins, sun damage, broken capillaries and birthmarks can all be removed, without trace in some instances, with laser-beam therapy.' He sounded as if he were reading it from a brochure.

The silence that fell was so heavy she felt it like a crushing weight against her chest. She could hardly breathe for the pressure, her lungs feeling as if they were full of lead instead of oxygen.

'S-so…' she moistened her parched lips '…so what you're saying is you…you had a birthmark and…and h-had it removed?'

He nodded again. 'I wouldn't have bothered except a mate of mine set up a cosmetic surgery practice with a sclerotherapy clinic attached. Strawberry birthmarks are harder to remove if they're not attended to while the person is young. The birthmark develops nodules over time which have to be surgically removed, hence the tiny scars.'

The silence was thrumming in Amelia's ears. Her head

seemed to be full of it, making it difficult for her to think, let alone speak.

'Alex…I don't know how to tell you this but the prince who was kidnapped thirty-four years ago had a birthmark. A very distinctive birthmark.'

He looked at her without speaking, but she could see the way his throat tightened, the muscles contracting as if he were trying to swallow something too big to go down.

'Y-you know what this means…don't you?' she finally managed to ask as a sinking feeling settled in the middle of her stomach.

'I'm not sure it means anything,' he said in an offhand manner. 'Lots of people have birthmarks.'

'But don't you see how it all makes sense?' she asked. 'You were adopted—a late adoption at two years of age, the exact age of the prince when he was supposedly murdered. You even had the same Christian name. People have remarked on your resemblance to Antonio and Marco Fierezza from the moment you stepped on the island. Don't you see it all adds up?'

'My birth certificate documents—'

'Birth certificates can be forged!' she interrupted him, her eyes wide with anguish. 'Especially when lots of money changes hands.'

'You seem to know an awful lot about all this,' he observed with a slight narrowing of his eyes. 'You said someone told you the prince wasn't murdered. Was that person by any chance your father?'

Amelia felt the trickle of ice-cold dread make its way down her spine. She had desperately wanted to protect her family from the fallout from all of this, but how could she now? Alex had a right to know the truth. He had been denied all of his other rights since the age of two when he had been snatched from his parents. How could she stand by now and not tell him everything she knew?

'Yes,' she said on the back end of a wobbly sigh. 'He knows he's dying. My brother told him of the rumours down at the port. My father wants to see you.'

Alex blew out a breath and ran a hand through his hair as he began to pace the room. 'This is totally surreal. I can't believe any of this.'

'I know it must be hard for you to grasp…but it's real, Alex. It has to be. It all adds up.' Tears burned in her eyes as she realised that what she was about to say would permanently sever any chance of a relationship between them. Their two worlds were now even farther apart and could never be bridged.

'You aren't simply Dr Alex Hunter, the visiting surgeon from Australia.' She took a scalding breath and continued, 'You are His Royal Highness Prince Alessandro Fierezza of Niroli, the next in line to the throne.'

CHAPTER ELEVEN

'No,' ALEX said, stopping his pacing for a moment to face Amelia. 'No way. That's not going to happen. *No way.*'

'You can't escape it, Alex. That's why the king asked to see you. He must have suspected who you were but without proof couldn't tell you.'

'It will totally devastate my parents,' he said, beginning to pace once again, even more agitatedly this time. 'They will think they are in some way responsible for this.'

'How can they be held responsible?' she asked.

He turned around to face her again. 'My adoption was legal. I can't imagine for a moment that my parents would have settled for anything less than that. Sure, they wanted a child, but not someone else's, or at least not without that other person's permission.'

'The adoption probably was legal, or at least on the surface,' she said. 'My father said he'd had to pay dearly for it. It totally ruined him. That's why we've lived with so little for so long.'

'Nice to know there's been some sort of rough justice in all of this,' Alex said before he could restrain himself.

He saw the sudden slump of her slim shoulders and gave himself a mental kick. It was totally wrong that she'd had to suffer for her father's actions so long ago. She had nothing to do with this.

Or had she?

The suspicion crept towards him like a lurking shadow, stealthily consuming the sunlight of his belief in her innocence. What if she had known all along? Was that why she had agreed to go out with him, her little act of initial reluctance a ploy to keep him interested?

He looked down and saw tears sparkling in her eyes. 'You have every right to say that,' she said. 'My father took you away from everything that was rightfully yours.'

'Yeah, well, at least he didn't kill me,' he said, still trying to make up his mind about her. 'I guess I should be grateful for that.'

'He couldn't do it,' she said. 'He was given the order to do so but he just couldn't do it.'

'So he shipped me away, one imagines to Sicily, and got some papers doctored in order to send me to Australia.'

'I haven't asked him how he did it but I'm sure he will tell you. I don't expect you to forgive him...it would be hard for anyone to forgive such an action, but it's a thousand times worse for you have lost so much.'

Alex felt the see-saw of doubt tipping back the other way, making it hard for him to believe her capable of such complicity.

'I don't see it quite like that,' he said after a little pause. 'Or at least I haven't as yet. I have a wonderful family. I have wanted for nothing my whole childhood and adult life.'

She gave him an agonised look. 'Your biological parents were killed two years ago in a yachting accident. They went to their graves not knowing the truth about your existence. You can never meet them or talk to them now, even if you wanted to.'

He frowned as he took it all in. 'I hadn't thought about that.'

'There's more,' she went on. 'You have siblings. Your twin brother for one thing and two sisters. Can you imagine how thrilled they will be to know you are alive?'

He shook his head as if he still couldn't quite make sense of all she'd told him. 'This is going to take some getting used to. What's my kid sister going to say when she finds out her brother is a prince?'

'She will love you just the same. So will your adoptive parents. It doesn't change anything in that regard.'

He gave her an incredulous look. 'It changes everything, can't you see that? Damn it, Amelia, what the hell am I going to do? I have a life and a career back in Sydney. I don't belong here. I don't even speak Italian!'

'Language is not an issue—almost everyone speaks English now anyway. This is your rightful heritage, Alex. You can't ignore your right to the throne.

'The king is your grandfather,' she continued. 'It will bring him much joy to finally meet you, having believed for so long that his reluctance to pay the ransom for your return led to your death.'

Alex came back to her and took her hands in his, hoping his gut feeling was right in all this. 'How like you to think of the other innocents in all of this,' he said, watching her closely. 'Is that something the nuns taught you?'

'They taught me that forgiveness is not always clear-cut but it's essential to let go of the things you cannot change,' she said softly. 'It's sometimes the only thing you can do.'

'I can't change who I am.'

'No one wants you to.'

'You don't know that,' he said. 'I bet as soon as the palace officials hear about this there will be members of the press running about shoving cameras under my nose, people following me no doubt trying to kiss my feet or whatever it is that people do with royalty. I'll go crazy within days and then they *will* have to find a dungeon for me with a strait-jacket as well as ankle chains.'

'It might not be anything like that. I would assume for the sake of everyone's privacy that they will keep this quiet for a while. They'll want to make absolutely sure of everything before it is announced publicly. They will probably organise a DNA test to establish your identity once and for all.'

'You already said the island was rife with rumours,' he pointed out. 'How much worse will it be trying to do what I came here to do with everyone gawking at me as if I'm some sort of freak?'

Amelia let out a ragged sigh. 'I know this is hard… You'll get used to it in time.'

'And what about us?' he asked, his eyes coming back to pin hers.

She gave him a look of immeasurable sadness. 'There can be no "us" now. Surely you can see that?'

Alex let a little silence count the seconds as doubt and belief each jostled for position in his head.

'I can see no reason why I shouldn't live my life the way I want to,' he said. 'If I want to be involved with you or anybody then surely that's up to me, not someone else to decide.'

'My father is responsible for what happened,' she said. 'It would be unthinkable for you to be involved with me now. The palace will outlaw it as soon as they find out.'

'No one's going to tell me what I can and cannot do. Come on, Amelia, surely you're not going to fall for that rubbish? This is about you and me. We've got something going, a good thing. Don't let this other stuff get in the way.'

'It will always get in the way, Alex. This is not something you can brush to one side as if it's nothing. This is your birth-right, your heritage. You were born to this.'

'But I didn't grow up with any of this! How can I change my life now? I want to be a normal person. Damn it! I *am* a normal person. I make my own meals, I drive my own car, and I even do my own tax income forms. I would have a hard time accepting a knighthood let alone a royal throne.'

'You have to accept it!' she cried. 'You have to.'

'I'm not accepting anything until I know what exactly

happened to me when I was two. This could all be a mistake. There's no guarantee that any of this is true,' he said. 'We're going to visit your father and I'm not taking no for an answer.'

He reached for his keys and held open the door. 'Come on, let's get this over with.'

He didn't speak again until they were driving along the foothills to Amelia's cottage. 'I know you think I should come forward, Amelia, but don't forget I have to perform heart surgery on the king in a matter of days. I think it's better all round to continue to view him as a patient like any other, despite the fact that he may be my grandfather.'

Amelia could appreciate his point of view. It would make the surgery a lot more stressful if Alex was in some way emotionally involved with the patient. Surgeons were usually discouraged from operating on close relatives in case their clinical judgement was affected.

'Besides,' Alex continued, 'I want to investigate this myself before anyone else jumps to conclusions that may not be accurate. If it turns out to be true, then I'll have to cross that bridge when I come to it.'

'But how will you investigate it?'

'Firstly I want to talk to your father and get his angle on what happened, and then I'll get someone to run a check on my birth certificate and adoption details, which will no doubt take a week or two.'

'Will you tell your parents and sister?'

'Not at this stage,' he said, shifting the gears. 'For now this is between us and your father—no one else.'

Amelia sank back in her seat, her thoughts flying off in all directions.

'I mean it, Amelia,' he said, flicking a quick glance her way. 'I'm only here for a short time. I want this time we have together to be about us, not some myth about me being a long-lost prince.'

'But you are the prince,' she said softly. 'I just know you are.'

'Maybe, but princes can still be attracted to beautiful women, can't they?' he said.

She felt her heart give a painful contraction. 'Yes, they can, but it would be unwise to do so with a woman from a background such as mine.'

'I have no problem with your background,' he said. 'In fact I think it's one of the most enchanting things about you.'

She frowned at him. 'But my father is solely responsible for what happened to you! How can you even think of a relationship with me?'

One of his hands left the steering wheel to capture one of hers. She held her breath as he brought her hand up to his mouth, her stomach turning inside out when he placed his lips to her fingers in a soft-as-air kiss. 'That's why,' he said, and, keeping her hand in his, brought it to rest on the top of his thigh.

Amelia thought her father's cottage looked even tawdrier in the fading light of the evening as Alex parked his car under the trees a little while later. There was an unmistakable irony in its stark contrast from the castle they had visited a few hours earlier. It seemed to drive home all the more forcefully the inherent differences between their backgrounds. Even without the spectre of his royal status, Alex's childhood had still been leagues away from hers. She had never known the comfort of a well-tended home and reliable income to provide the standard of living he more or less had taken for granted. She felt sure he had never come home from school or university to a sink full of unwashed dishes, and dust like carpet on the floor.

She felt the shame rush through her as soon as Alex came up behind her when she opened the front door, imagining how he too would be making his own comparisons.

Her father looked up from his slumped position at the table, his bleary-eyed gaze widening when it encountered the tall figure carrying a doctor's bag who had followed Amelia inside.

'*Papà*, this is Dr Alex Hunter,' she said in a subdued tone.

Alex saw the older man's struggle to get to his feet and gently laid a hand on his shoulder. 'No, please don't get up.' He offered his hand. 'How do you do, Signor Vialli?'

Amelia could see the mortal fear on her father's already too-pale face. He choked back a hacking cough and gave Alex's outstretched hand a feeble shake, mumbling something inaudible in return.

'Your daughter tells me you've not been well,' Alex said, pulling out a chair and sitting beside him.

'I'm dying,' Aldo Vialli said. 'It's what I deserve.'

'There's no need to suffer unnecessarily,' Alex said. 'There are things we can do to help you through the difficult stages.'

'*Papà*, I've talked to Alex about what happened,' Amelia said.

Her father's eyes glazed with pain as another bout of coughing took over his emaciated form. She saw the sympathetic wince Alex tried to disguise, and she felt as if her heart had swelled to twice its size.

'Do you feel up to answering some questions for him?' she asked.

Her father looked at her. 'The birthmark?' he croaked.

Amelia nodded gravely. 'He had one but had it removed. It was as you described.'

Tears began to shine in Aldo Vialli's eyes as he faced Alex. 'I was supposed to kill you.... I could not do it....'

'Thank you,' Alex said with gracious sincerity.

Her father blinked back the tears. 'I never intended to get so involved, not in that way. I had to think of an alternative.... It was never my intention to bring such suffering on you or your family. But what is done is done, and cannot be undone.'

'I understand,' Alex said, wondering if he really did. He was feeling more than a little shell-shocked as he faced the man supposedly responsible for the bizarre circumstances that had led to his adoption. None of it seemed real. It was the stuff of Hollywood thrillers, not normal life. How could it be true? Sure, he'd been adopted at the age of two, but that didn't mean he was the king's grandson. There could be thousands of men his age who could just as easily fit the bill.

'You are so like your father,' Aldo choked out. 'It is my fault that you have not had the chance to meet him in person.'

'Nothing's been established as yet,' Alex said. 'There are legal channels that need to be investigated first. I know it all seems to fit, but what if I'm not who you think I am?'

'There is no doubt in my mind,' Aldo said. 'You had the birthmark that, if nothing else, brands you as Alessandro Fierezza.'

'Look, to make things a little clearer in my head I'd like to know a few more details, if you feel up to telling me?' Alex said.

'Of…course,' Aldo said in between another hacking cough. 'I will tell you…'

Amelia sat in silence as her father relayed the events of thirty-four years ago, the picture he painted so painful to hear, she had trouble keeping her emotions at bay.

It was clear to Amelia after his confession that her father was exhausted. His skin had taken on a clammy sheen and his eyes had flickered once too often with increasing pain. His breathing was laboured and when he turned to spit some mucus into his old rag her stomach clenched at the sight of how bright the blood was.

'*Papà*, would you like Alex to look at you now?' she asked. 'He might be able to do something to ease your suffering.'

After another bout of gut-wrenching coughs, Alex exchanged a glance with Amelia before he bent to his bag on the floor and retrieved his stethoscope.

'Amelia, help take off your father's shirt so I can examine his chest,' he directed.

Once the shirt was removed Alex looked at the degree of

chest expansion as Aldo took in a few breaths and then percussed the chest and listened with his stethoscope.

'You have a very large pleural effusion on the right side of your chest, Signor Vialli. That is making it hard for you to breathe, and may be precipitating a lot of the coughing. I may be able to at least temporarily relieve some of your symptoms by draining off the fluid with a needle,' he said.

'I am not going to go to the hospital. I will die here in my house, not in some institution, where everyone will know who I am, what I have done,' Aldo said.

'Signor Vialli—' Alex's voice deepened with professional authority '—performing a pleural drainage here would be too risky. For one thing there's the risk of infection, and secondly there's the possibility of me pricking the lung and causing a pneumothorax —puncturing the lung, I mean. If that were to happen, you could be worse off. We could go to the hospital now and do it without anyone but the night staff knowing about it. The procedure is relatively simple and will give you a few weeks' relief.'

'*Papà*, surely it's worth letting Alex try to help you,' Amelia pleaded.

Aldo let out a broken sigh. 'Very well…I will have the procedure done…but I do not want to stay in hospital.'

'That shouldn't be necessary if all goes well,' Alex said and helped the ill man from the chair, taking most of his weight on his arm.

Amelia sent him a grateful glance as they made their way out to Alex's car, her father's coughing increasing with every shuffling step he took.

The drive down to the Free Hospital was mostly silent. Alex tried once or twice to make conversation with Signor Vialli, but it was obvious both breathing and talking caused him too much discomfort.

Their arrival at the hospital was met with some slight

surprise on the part of the night staff nurse on duty, but once Alex explained what he intended to do she organised the equipment for him and led him to one of the treatment bays and drew the curtains around them.

Amelia helped her father into a sitting position on the bed at Alex's direction and supported his leaning-forward position by holding his shoulders.

Alex pulled on a pair of sterile gloves after washing and drying his hands, and, using the swabs from the disposable dressing tray, cleaned an area on the right side of Aldo's chest, his ribs clearly obvious because of marked weight loss.

'I'm going to put in some local anaesthetic so it doesn't hurt too much,' Alex explained.

He injected ten milligrams of one per cent xylocaine with adrenaline into the area for the pleural tap. Then, taking a fourteen gauge IV canula, to the end of which he attached a three-way tap and a twenty-mil syringe, Alex punctured the right pleural space just lateral to the tip of the right scapula, and aspirated 20ml of blood-stained pleural fluid. He then withdrew the IV needle, leaving the plastic canula in the pleural cavity, and aspirated the pleural effusion 20ml at a time, discarding each aspirate by using the three-way tap, into the stainless steel container the nurse had provided.

'You may feel like coughing as the fluid comes out, Signor Vialli. Try to suppress coughing as much as possible, just do little coughs if you have to, and try to keep as still as possible while I remove the fluid,' Alex said.

For Amelia, it seemed as though the fluid would never end; so far Alex had removed two litres of blood-stained effusion. But at about three litres, the pleural cavity was drained, and Alex removed the needle, taping a dressing over the puncture site.

'How does that feel? Can you breathe any easier?' Alex asked.

Aldo took a deep breath, and let it out slowly. This time there was no hacking cough.

'This is much better, Dr Hunter. I can breathe freely again. How long will this last?' Aldo asked.

'I can't really say,' Alex said. 'The fluid may come back very quickly, and you'll be thirsty and have to drink. Or it may accumulate very slowly, maybe over a few weeks. When much of the fluid comes back, I can drain it off again.'

'Do you think there will be any problems from the tap, Alex, infection or a pneumothorax?' Amelia asked, moving just out of her father's hearing.

Alex moved back to listen to Aldo's chest again with his stethoscope. 'The air entry is much better, and there isn't clinical evidence of a pneumothorax. I'll give him some sample packs of amoxicillin. He should start those now, and we'll get some more from the pharmacy tomorrow.'

'Thank you, Dr Hunter,' Aldo said as Amelia helped him to his feet once more.

'No problem.' Alex smiled. 'Let's get you home and into bed.'

Once her father was settled back at the cottage Amelia walked out with Alex to his car to see him off.

'Your father should really be in hospital,' he said as he drew her closer. 'He's in a bad way and it's only going to get worse.'

'I know.' She let out a tiny sigh and looked up at him. 'Thank you for what you did for him tonight.'

'I didn't do much.'

'You did more than you realise,' she said. 'Apart from relieving the pressure in his chest, you listened to his reasons for doing what he did without judgement and yet you of all people should be angry. He took your childhood away and exchanged it for another.'

'Maybe, but who's to say the one I got in exchange wasn't as good? I don't have a single bad memory of my childhood, that's more than what most people can say these days. It might have been a completely different story living a royal life. Who knows? I might have become horrendously overindulged and totally obnoxious.'

She smiled at his self-effacing humour. 'I can't imagine you ever being any such thing.'

He lifted her hand to his face and pressed a soft kiss to her palm, his eyes still locked to hers. 'You didn't like me the first time you met me, though, did you?'

'I didn't know you the first time I met you.'

'And you do now?' he asked after a protracted silence.

'I know you're a very special person....'

He narrowed his eyes at her playfully. 'If you mention the *P* word again I won't be answerable to the consequences. As far as I'm concerned I'm still Alex Hunter. Even if someone hands me a pedigree several centuries long I will still always feel like Alex Hunter, no one else.'

'But you'll have to face it soon,' she said with a troubled frown.

'Not yet.' He pulled her closer, his hands settling on her hips. 'Let's just be two ordinary people for a little while longer.'

'But the king should be told.'

'He will be told, but not right now. He's not well, for a start, and the shock of it could trigger a heart attack. I'd like to see him come through the procedure first. And anyway, I still have work to do at the Free Hospital. Can you imagine what would happen to that if I suddenly put my hand up for the throne? I came here to be a cardiac surgeon, not a prince. Once my work is completed I will have to face the issues surrounding my parentage, but until that time I'd rather just be me.'

She gave him a shadowed smile. 'I have spent most of my life wishing I was someone else. When I was a little girl I used to dream of being rescued out of poverty. I would imagine someone coming up here and informing me I had been mistakenly swapped at birth and that I no longer had to play with dolls made out of paper and sticks but real ones, ones that looked like the princess I felt I was really meant to be.'

His eyes were very dark as they held hers. 'I know what's happened might seem like a fairy tale to others, but let me tell you it's not. I guess I'm trying to keep my head by looking at this from a clinical distance. Although I met the king and some of my supposed siblings earlier this evening they felt like strangers to me. They still feel like strangers.'

'You have the same blood running in your veins.'

'Genetics is only a fraction of the equation,' he said. 'The nurture of a child is far more of an indicator than DNA profiles. I can't explain it any other way but I *feel* like the son of Clara and Giles Hunter. I always have, even though I've always been aware of being adopted.'

'I'm sure your adoptive parents will want you to do what's right for you. They will not be thinking of themselves but of what is best for you.'

He gave her a crooked smile. 'Like you, huh?'

She held his gaze, even though her heart felt as if it were being squeezed. 'What I want doesn't come into it at all.'

He frowned at her tone. 'What is it you want, Amelia?'

She looked up into his face, her eyes shining with moisture. 'I want you to be who you are called to be. It's your life and only you can make that choice.'

'For now this is my choice.' His voice was gravel rough and deep as his mouth came down towards hers. 'To be with you.'

But for how long? Amelia thought sadly as she lost herself in his kiss. It was too easy to forget about tomorrow when the heat and fire of the moment blazed so blindingly today.

Alex lifted his mouth from hers a few breathless minutes later. 'Have dinner with me tomorrow night,' he said. 'Bring some casual clothes and bathers with you to work so you can change at my house. We'll go on a sunset picnic to one of the beaches away from all the crowds. I don't want people staring at us.'

'I'm not sure…' She hesitated. 'My father—'

'Will want you to spend time with me,' he assured her. 'After all, he owes me, right? If I want to take his daughter out, then what can he say?'

'Good point,' she said with a smile.

He grazed his knuckles over her cheek. 'You see what dastardly means I have to resort to in order to get you to come out with me? I've never had to work quite so hard before. You are doing serious and very likely irreversible damage to my fragile male ego.'

'I don't think your ego has ever been in any sort of danger.'

He gave her a quick grin. 'No, you're right. Not while you keep looking at me with those big hazel eyes of yours.' He dropped a swift kiss to the end of her nose. 'Till tomorrow, little elf.'

'Till tomorrow,' she echoed softly as she watched the fiery red glare of his tail-lights disappear into the darkness of the night.

CHAPTER TWELVE

AMELIA couldn't wait for her shift to be over the next day. She checked her watch for the tenth time in as many minutes, scoring yet another speculative look from Lucia.

'You seem very impatient to be out of here,' the nurse observed. 'Could it be that you have something special planned for this evening?'

'No…no, nothing special.'

Lucia smiled knowingly. 'I don't think Dr Hunter would like to hear you describe your date with him as "nothing special".'

Amelia stared at her. 'He *told* you about that?'

'Not in as many words,' Lucia said. 'I just put two and two together. I saw the way he looked at you every time he was on the ward today. I met him in the canteen and asked him how he was enjoying the island and whether he'd been to any of the beaches. He said he was taking a friend this evening for a sunset picnic.'

'So you immediately thought that friend was me?'

Lucia's smile widened. 'It was a good guess, I thought, and, judging by the colour of your cheeks—spot on.'

Amelia considered denying it just for the sake of it, but she knew Lucia well enough to know she wouldn't be fooled.

'You went to the palace with him last night, didn't you?' Lucia said.

'How *do* you find out all this stuff?'

Lucia grinned. 'I have connections.'

'Well, tell your connections to mind their own business,' Amelia said. 'I don't want the whole island talking about one casual date.'

'Two if you count the other night, which, young lady, I am quite peeved that you didn't tell me about.' She leaned closer and added, 'Did he kiss you?'

Amelia frowned. 'I'm not going to answer that.'

'No, you don't need to as your face just did it for you,' Lucia said with another cheeky grin.

Amelia sent her a reproving glance. 'Don't go ordering the invitations and caterers. He's only on the island for a month.'

'So who's counting the days?'

'I'm just being realistic,' Amelia said. 'Besides, he comes from a totally different world. We have hardly anything in common.'

'He's a man—you're a woman. That's all that matters,' Lucia said. 'You of all people deserve to have a little fling. Who cares how long it lasts?'

I care, Amelia thought as she reached for her bag. *I care too much.*

Alex watched as she came towards him in the hospital car park, her small bag in one hand and a worried frown disturbing the elfin perfection of her face.

He eased himself away from the car and took her bag, smiling down at her. 'Hi.'

She looked up at him with a nervous smile. 'Hi.'

'Are you OK?'

She moistened her mouth. 'Yes.'

'Hey—' he pushed up her chin '—I'm just Alex tonight. Got that?'

She gave him a rueful look. 'Yes, and I'm a princess,' she said.

He laughed. 'Yeah, that's right. You are.'

'Alex…'

'Stop worrying about it,' he said as he helped her into the car. 'I've got it all under control.'

She waited until he was behind the driver's wheel before speaking. 'Have you found out anything yet?'

He started the engine and backed out of the space, swinging a quick glance her way as he drove out of the hospital grounds. 'I have someone working on it as we speak. But just for tonight let's forget all about it, OK?'

'If that's what you'd prefer.'

He sent her a warm smile that momentarily suppressed the dark shadows she'd seen in his eyes. 'It's what I prefer,' he said.

Amelia sat in silence as he drove the short distance to his cottage, her senses on high alert. She could smell the sexy musk of his body intermingled with the lingering fragrance of his citrus aftershave, and her skin began to prickle all over at the thought of feeling his kiss, his touch and his intimate caresses.

How would it feel to have his arms around her, his skin on her skin, his body within hers again?

She knew their relationship was being conducted on borrowed time, but the sense of urgency only heightened her attraction to him and she wondered if he felt it too.

She sneaked a look at him as he drove, his long-fingered hands steady on the wheel, his face showing nothing of the inner turmoil he surely must be going through.

Alex caught her looking at him. 'I hope you're not having second thoughts.'

'About what?'

'About us.'

She looked down at her hands. 'This is temporary, Alex. You and I both know that.'

'You're putting up obstacles that don't need to be there.'

'But they *are* there,' she insisted. 'Pretending they're not isn't going to make them go away.'

His jaw tightened. 'I don't want to talk about it tonight, remember? Tonight we're just a man and a woman who are attracted to each other.'

'I'm not denying that, but I think we both should be realistic.'

'You're being fatalistic, not realistic,' he said.

'I'm trying to protect myself from hurt.'

He let out a deep sigh and reached for her hand, bringing it up to his mouth to press a soft kiss to her fingertips. 'I don't want to hurt you, Amelia.'

'You won't be able to avoid it.'

He met her troubled gaze. 'I will do everything in my power to avoid it. Trust me.'

Could she risk her heart another time? She had spent the last eleven years regretting the one and only time she had let her guard slip.

'Trust me?' he said again.

She gave him a tremulous smile. 'I know I'm going to regret this, but I do trust you.'

'Good girl,' he said. 'Now we're getting somewhere.'

Amelia used the bathroom to change out of her uniform while Alex organised the picnic and within a few minutes they were on their way to a beach at the far end of Santa Fiera where the sandy shore was less frequented by tourists.

'How about a swim first?' Alex suggested once he'd laid a blanket on the sand and anchored it with the picnic basket.

'You go. I'll sit here and watch for a while,' Amelia said.

Alex could sense her self-consciousness. In spite of the evening's warmth she was dressed in a shapeless cotton shift that looked at least three sizes too big. He could also see the thick straps of the dark one-piece bathing costume she was wearing, its unflattering lines suggesting she hadn't been to the beach in a very long time.

He wondered if he'd done the right thing in bringing her here, but he'd figured that at least on a picnic she hadn't had to worry about dressing up. Besides, he wanted time with her away from other people and their increasingly speculative stares.

He still couldn't get his head around the circumstances surrounding his infancy. At first he had hoped it was all a mistake but the investigations he'd set in motion so far had led him to suspect the opposite. The legal people he'd engaged to work on it had already come across one or two discrepancies in the paperwork regarding his adoption and had hinted that there could be even more. He couldn't bear the thought of informing his parents of what he'd discovered. He knew it would hurt them immeasurably to find they had inadvertently adopted a child who had had parents who had loved him and desperately longed for his return.

Alex felt as if he was in limbo; he couldn't go back and neither could he go forward until he knew for sure what was expected of him. But for the time being he had a responsibility to get the king through his surgery; that was a main priority— everything else would have to wait.

He had even shelved his earlier concerns about Amelia's family connections, unable to accept her as anything other than a young woman who was learning how to live again after a bitter let-down, not unlike his own. He had found it hard to become involved with anyone since his break-up with Sarah and instead had thrown himself into work as a distraction. The hurt he had felt about her affair with another man had niggled at him for so long and yet when he was with Amelia he complétely forgot about it.

He let out a small sigh as he walked down towards the ocean. The water was refreshing after the heat of the day and he struck out vigorously, hoping to exercise some of his tension away.

* * *

Amelia sat on the sand hugging her bent knees, watching as Alex swam further than most people could walk. He was a picture of health and vitality, his tanned, muscular body carving through the water like a streamlined torpedo.

She couldn't help a little sigh of envy. She had never learned to swim with any proficiency. Her family circumstances had ruled out swimming lessons during her childhood and as she'd grown older she'd become too embarrassed to admit to her inability.

Her mother's bathing costume felt scratchy and uncomfortable and she longed to remove it. This end of the beach was deserted, but the thought of sitting next to Alex with nothing on but her thin shift was too disturbing.

She saw him make his way towards her, his strong legs slicing through the shallows, the crystal droplets of salt-water making his whole body glisten in the evening sunlight.

'Come on in,' he said, offering her a hand.

'No…I'm fine here.'

'Come on, Amelia. It's not the least bit cold.'

'Please…I'd rather not.' She hugged her knees even tighter.

He frowned as he joined her on the sand. 'What's the problem?'

'Nothing.'

He grazed her cheek with the back of his fingers. 'Look at me, Amelia.'

She met his dark gaze and suddenly found herself confessing, 'I…I can't swim.'

His eyes softened like melted chocolate. 'That's nothing to be ashamed of. It can take a long time to learn to swim properly.'

She chewed at her lip. 'I've never had lessons.'

'Well, then, now's a perfect time to start. I can teach you. It's like riding a bike—once you learn, you learn for life.'

He got to his feet and hauled her upright before she could protest. 'Take off your dress and let's go in to our knees.'

Amelia self-consciously wriggled out of her cotton dress and followed him to the water's edge, stepping into the water tentatively, her toes looking for stability in the shifting sand. After a moment or two she felt more secure and went in a little farther, this time up to her thighs as she held tightly to Alex's hand.

'That's great. Now let's go to your waist,' he said.

She took a deep breath and walked in a little farther, wincing as the water swirled around her middle and almost made her lose her balance.

'Easy does it,' he said, holding her waist with his hands from behind.

Amelia could feel his body behind her like a strong wall of muscle, his legs braced against the frothing surf. It was the most erotic sensation having his hard body so close to hers. She could even feel the beginnings of his arousal, the gradual thickening of his body, a heady reminder of all that set them apart as man and woman. Her breasts felt tight and heavy, her legs felt insecure and weak and her heart began to race.

They were totally alone on the beach.

They were practically skin on skin.

All she had to do was turn around and his mouth would find hers....

She turned around and met his glittering gaze, her throat locking up at the desire she could see reflected there. He brought her closer so there was no room, not even for water to separate them.

His head came down, his mouth capturing hers in a searing kiss that swept her away on a rushing tide of rapture. It felt so good to be crushed against him, his tongue swooping and meeting hers, his body pressing urgently against her.

She felt his hands leave her hips to explore the curves of her breasts, his thumbs rolling over each tight nipple until she was mindless with sensation. Without taking his mouth off hers, he pushed the straps of her bathing costume aside to access her naked breasts with the warmth of his palms. The feel of his hands caressing her stole her breath and made her legs wobble beneath her.

The pulse of the ocean around them only added to the swirl of sensual feelings swamping her; no part of her was unaffected by his touch. With her bathers practically around her waist she knew she should be calling some sort of halt to this onslaught of sensuality, but there was nothing she could do to pull away.

His mouth left hers and began to kiss its way down the side of her neck on a slow but steady passage towards her aching, swollen breasts. She could feel her skin tightening all over in tiny goose-bumps at the erotic press of his lips as they made their way down…down…

'Oh…' She let out a hoarse gasp as his hot mouth closed over her engorged nipple, the rasp of his tongue turning her insides to liquid. She clutched at his head to hold herself upright, her breath coming in stunted little bursts as he suckled on each of her breasts in turn.

He brought his mouth back to hers and her loose bathers slipped even farther so that she could feel his erection on the bare skin of her quivering stomach. It was shockingly intimate, but she couldn't stop herself from reaching down and tracing his rigid contours with the tips of her fingers, tentatively at first and then with increasing boldness as his throaty groans filled her mouth.

His kiss became more urgent, the mastery of his tongue leaving her in no doubt of his expertise as a lover. She could almost feel him inside her again as she stood there in the rocking ocean with him, his body burning into hers with unmistakable purpose. She had never felt anything like the passion filling her; it consumed her totally, leaving no room for common sense.

Alex tore his mouth off hers and looked down at her with passion-glazed eyes, his chest rising and falling as he struggled to regain control. 'I guess I'm not the world's best swimming teacher, huh?'

She gave him a shy smile and covered her naked breasts with her hands. 'I don't know about that—I certainly felt like I was floating there for a while.'

He smiled. 'Me too, especially when you did that little thing with your fingers.'

She felt her colour rise and bit her bottom lip in embarrassment. 'I don't know what came over me.'

'Hey, do you hear me complaining?' He removed her hands from her breasts, running his dark gaze over her hungrily.

'Alex…'

'Mmm?' He pressed a burning kiss to the top of her right breast, so close to her aching nipple she could barely think.

She squirmed and tried again. 'My…er…bathers are slipping.'

She felt his smile on the side of her other breast. 'Want a hand to take them off?' he asked.

She clutched at his head again, her voice totally breathless as his tongue rasped over her puckered nipple. 'N-no…no…someone might see us.'

He lifted his head and glanced around them. 'There's no one around for miles. Come on, if you take yours off, I'll take off mine.'

She stared at him in alarm. 'You're surely not serious?'

He gave her a stomach-flipping smile. 'As your very own personal swimming coach I insist you get a feel for the water. Believe me, it makes the world of difference. Besides, that costume of yours is like a diving weight belt. You'd sink to the bottom in two strokes.'

Amelia hesitated for a moment. What harm would it do? she wondered. Wasn't it about time she learned to put the past

aside and enjoy life for once? Lucia was right: Alex was a man
and she was a woman. This was the twenty-first century;
women were entitled to have temporary lovers. It didn't mean
they were promiscuous or bad people. It was natural to feel
desire; it was even healthy.

She took an unsteady breath and pushed the bathers down
with her hands and stepped out of them. She felt Alex's gaze
sweeping over her and her heart kicked in response to the
almost palpable desire she could feel coming off him.

'Now it's your turn,' she said huskily.

His gaze locked down on hers challengingly. 'You do it.'

She swallowed and squeaked, 'Me?'

He nodded.

She moistened her mouth and reached blindly with
unsteady hands for the waist of his black bathers, her fingers
curling into the fabric for purchase as she pulled them down
past his lean hips. She felt him spring against her nakedness,
the length and strength of him sending shock waves of delight
between her legs. She could feel her womb pulsing with need,
her whole body coming alive with escalating desire.

The wild sea air crawled with tension as he brought his
hands to her hips, gently pulling her against him, his hardened
length slipping between her legs in an erotically teasing
embrace that sent her senses into uncontrollable mayhem.

She raised herself on tiptoe to accommodate him, her
breath rushing out of her when he probed her intimately. She
felt the separation of her tender flesh as he surged forwards,
his deep, rumbling groan of pleasure as he filled her drowning
out the breathless gasp of her own.

His movements quickened, carrying her with him on a
roller coaster of feeling as her sensitive nerves responded
with increasing fervour to each of his determined thrusts. She
felt her body tingling as it steadily climbed towards the
summit of release, the inner muscles clamping on his thick-

ness made slippery with the dew of her desire. His mouth crushed hers once more, his hot breath filling her as he plunged again and again until she was hovering in the balance—the pleasure she craved was close, but not quite close enough. She whimpered against his lips, unable to express her need, but in the end she didn't need to; he felt it for himself. She quivered against his searching fingers, the engorged pearl of her womanhood responding with a heady rush, triggering a volley of panting cries from her throat as the waves of delight crashed in and over her. Her body rocked and shuddered against his until she felt him, too, tumble into the abyss of pleasure with deep, pumping thrusts that nudged her womb and made her skin prickle all over with sensation.

Alex gradually eased himself away, his hands still holding her to counteract the swell of the ocean. 'I guess you're not going to believe me when I tell you I didn't really intend for that to happen,' he said with a wry grimace, 'or at least not without protection.'

Her eyes clouded and her cheeks went a delicate shade of pink as she bent down to retrieve her bathers. 'It was just as much my fault as yours,' she said as she wriggled back into them.

'It was no one's fault,' he said, holding on to her arm to steady her. 'I guess sooner or later I knew it was going to be like this.'

She looked up at him. 'Y-you did?'

'Sure I did. It's called chemistry.' He smiled at her as he took her hand and led her to the picnic blanket on the sand.

Amelia curled up beside him with a sigh of contentment, his arms holding her loosely as they watched the waves rolling to the shore. She pressed a kiss to his neck, the salt of his skin and the sea making her lips tingle.

'You must be getting hungry,' Alex said, dropping a swift, hard kiss to her mouth.

'What makes you say that?' she asked with a twinkling smile.

'You're starting to gnaw on me.'

'You don't like the feel of my mouth on you?'

He pushed her back down and covered her with his body, a teasing smile playing at the corners of his mouth. 'Do you hear me complaining?'

'I guess not,' she breathed as his lips claimed hers in a searing kiss.

CHAPTER THIRTEEN

THE first stars were in the sky when Amelia surfaced from the sensual haven of Alex's arms.

'Are you cold?' he asked as he handed her a glass of wine.

'No, I'm fine.' She toyed with the glass for a moment before looking up at him. 'Alex…this thing between us…this chemistry you spoke of…don't you mean lust?'

'Lust sounds a bit shallow and transient to me,' he said.

'But this *is* transient…'

'That subject is off limits, remember? This is for now, Amelia. We'll take it one day at a time and enjoy what happens.'

'It's so easy for men to cast aside the practicalities,' she said. 'Sex is just sex for men—it's much more emotionally complicated for women.'

'That's a sweeping generalisation that does a lot of men a disservice,' he said. 'I know you've had a bad case of lover let-down, but not all men are after a one night stand or brief fling. I haven't had a one-night stand in my life and my shortest relationship lasted two years. It broke up about this time last year.'

'Were you in love with her?' she asked.

His eyes moved away from hers as he picked up his glass again. 'Yes, I loved her in my own way. I guess if I was honest with myself there had always been something missing in our relationship, but I chose to ignore it until it was too late. She'd been having an affair with a guy behind my back.' His brows came together slightly. 'She's married to him now and expecting his baby.'

Amelia wondered if that was why he had charged headlong into his relationship with her, out of a sense of loss. It made sense in a way, the holiday romance to dull the pain of rejection, especially since the woman he had loved had moved on with her life without him. She couldn't help wondering if his easygoing attitude covered much deeper hurt.

'I don't suppose a good convent girl like you would happen to be on the pill?' he asked after a moment or two of silence.

She almost choked on her mouthful of wine. 'I…um…I…'

His mouth tilted. 'That appears to be a straight-out no.'

She gnawed her bottom lip as she thought of their unprotected coupling. 'I didn't think…'

'Don't worry,' he said. 'I haven't got anything other than rampant fertility to threaten you with.'

Her eyes flew to his, her mouth dropping open. 'Isn't that bad enough?'

He gave a casual shrug and reached for his wine. 'Contrary to what people think, a woman is only fertile for about two days of every monthly cycle.'

She looked at him closely, trying to read his expression. 'Today could be one of the days,' she pointed out. 'What then?'

He held her gaze for several pulsing seconds. 'Would it be a problem for you?' he asked.

She gaped at him. 'Of course it would be a problem for me!'

'You're thirty years old,' he said. 'Aren't you hearing any ticking yet?'

She frowned at him. 'I suppose by that you're referring to my biological clock?'

'Every woman's got one even if she says she hasn't.' He turned to look out to sea and added, 'My ex-girlfriend always strenuously denied it because she sensed I wasn't ready for kids, but within no time after replacing me she was waving a blue dipstick in the air.'

Amelia felt her jaw tightening. 'I suppose that's why you've singled me out? Who better to knock up than a naïve left-on-the-shelf thirty-year-old woman whom you no doubt assumed would be far too grateful to notice the insincerity of your stupid proposal.' She tossed the contents of her glass to the sand and got to her feet and glared down at him furiously. 'How dare you toy with me in such a way?'

He stood up and frowned back at her. 'I was doing no such thing.'

Her eyes flashed at him. 'I don't believe you.'

'That's your choice,' he said in a hardened tone.

'I can see why your girlfriend left you,' she said. 'No woman wants to have a child with a man who refuses to grow up.'

'And I suppose you've got maturity down to an art form, have you?' he retorted with a touch of spite. 'You've spent the last eleven years running away from life. Don't tell me I haven't grown up when you've hidden away from everything that's adult.'

'I suppose it's adult to pretend things you don't feel to achieve your ends, is it?' she shot back.

His eyes blazed with growing anger. 'I haven't pretended anything. I've made my motives more than clear.'

She gave a mocking laugh. 'Oh, yes, indeed you have. From the first moment I met you your motives were blatantly obvious.'

'Would you care to explain that comment?'

She sent him a paint-stripping look. 'You don't need me to spell it out. Besides, you've already achieved your goal, haven't you? The little seduction routine worked, didn't it? I fell for it as you intended me to.'

'I don't deny I wanted to make love with you, and if you're honest with yourself you'll admit the same. You wanted me too, Amelia, so don't do that outraged little virginal routine with me. It just won't work.'

She stamped her foot on the sand. 'Take me home this instant.'

His lip curled insolently. 'I will when I'm good and ready.'

She let out a furious breath and, scooping up her things off the sand, turned for the twinkling lights of Santa Fiera in the distance.

'I would advise against walking all that way in the dark,' Alex called out after her.

'I'll take a chance on it,' she flung back at him.

He let out a frustrated sigh and followed her, his long legs swiftly closing the distance. He snagged one of her arms and turned her round to face him, deftly dodging her hand as it swung up for his face. 'Oh, no, you don't,' he warned as he captured her hand on its second attempt.

'If you don't let me go I'll scream,' she threatened, her chest heaving with rage.

'If you scream I'll kiss you until you shut up.'

Her eyes narrowed into slits. 'If you kiss me I'll bite you!'

He suddenly laughed and tugged her closer. 'I can hardly wait,' he said and covered her mouth with his.

Amelia opened her teeth to bite him but his tongue slipped through and found hers, taking her breath away as well as her urge to fight. She felt herself go weak in his arms, her legs softening until she was only remaining upright because he was holding her so tightly. Her head spun with every bold flick of his tongue against hers, the movement so deliciously evocative of what they had experienced earlier she could feel her lower body turning to liquid all over again. She leaned into him unashamedly, her pelvis on fire where his body pressed against her.

He lifted his mouth from hers and looked down at her with a teasing glint in his eyes. 'Are you still angry with me?'

She pursed her mouth at him. 'Furious.'

'Do you still want me to take you home straight away or can I tempt you back into sharing a picnic fit for a prince?'

Her mouth opened but she closed it again.

'I guess that wasn't such a great choice of words,' he acceded wryly.

Her shoulders gave a little slump. 'It was a mistake for me to come with you tonight.'

'I shouldn't have mentioned the *P* word.'

'What about the other *P* word?' she asked. 'What if I did become pregnant?'

'As long as you were happy, I'd be happy,' he said. 'We could get married straight away and live snappily ever after.'

She rolled her eyes at him. 'Very funny.'

'We'd be a great couple. I can see it now—every single fight would end up in bed.'

'Only because you don't fight fair.'

'Look who's talking.' He slung a casual arm around her shoulders and led her back towards the picnic blanket. 'You were the one threatening to bite me and you tried to throw me a right hook.'

'You made me angry.'

'I like it when you're angry,' he said. 'You turn me on.'

She glanced up at him. 'Did your ex-girlfriend ever make you angry?'

He met her eyes briefly before turning away to open the picnic basket. 'That's another *P* word I'd like to stay away from tonight—past lovers.'

'You're not over her, are you?' she said as he handed her a plate.

His eyes came back to hers. 'I would be a shallow sort of bloke if I could walk away after two years without some regrets. But I am over her. I hardly even think of her now.'

Amelia felt something heavy begin to weigh her chest down. 'What do you regret?'

He shifted his lips from side to side as if thinking about it. 'I don't know... Maybe I should have been more spontaneous. I worked too hard and forgot how to have fun. I woke up three weeks after Sarah left me for another man and realised I had to loosen up, you know, laugh at life a bit more.'

'So you suddenly found yourself a sense of humour?'

'No, not really. I guess I've always been a happy-go-lucky sort of guy, but years of study and long hours and being responsible for patients' lives took its toll. I was heading towards a total burn-out and Sarah giving me the boot was the wake-up call I needed.'

'Do you ever see her?'

'What would be the point? It's over. She has a new life and I don't belong in it.'

'She's going to kick herself when she finds out she knocked back a prince,' she said without thinking.

His expression clouded as he rummaged for cutlery and napkins. 'As far as I see it, it's a title, not a description of who I am as a person.'

'I know, but people will still have certain expectations.'

'I have to live up to my own expectations, not those of other people.'

'This is really hard for you, isn't it?' she asked after a taut little silence.

He met her gaze, his small smile slightly skewed. 'How would you feel to suddenly find out you weren't who you thought you were?'

'You're still Alex Hunter.'

'But for how long?' he asked.

Amelia sighed as she reached for his hand and gave it a little squeeze. 'It's still a secret,' she tried to reassure him. 'No one needs to know a thing until you feel ready to tell them who you are.'

His dark eyes became shadowed. 'I'd just like another

week or two,' he said. 'That will be enough time to get the king through the surgery and my work commitments at the Free Hospital seen to. After that I guess it will have to be dealt with in some way or another, but I can't help feeling it's going to be hard on your father.'

'I know. My father wants the truth to be told, but I don't think he realises yet the implications for him. He'll be charged and no doubt sent to prison.'

He began to stroke her cheek with his fingers. 'You realise he hasn't got much time left, don't you?'

She nodded silently.

'At least this way you get the chance to say goodbye,' he said, dropping his hand and looking out to sea again. 'So many people don't.'

Amelia looked at him, wondering if he was thinking of his biological parents. It was hard to tell from his expression, but she couldn't help feeling he was trying to come to terms with his new-found identity instead of pushing the reality of it away as he had insisted on doing earlier.

'Alex…can I ask you something?'

He turned back to look at her. 'Of course.'

'I want to know what your intentions are in regards to me.'

'I thought I'd made it pretty clear a few minutes ago exactly what my intentions are.'

She bit her lip momentarily. 'I can't help feeling you're doing the whole rebound thing.'

A shutter came down over his face as he turned to look out at the ocean. 'I'm over that part of my life,' he said. 'I told you—I don't even think of her any more.'

Amelia wondered if that was true. She had noticed a tension in him every time his ex-partner was mentioned, as if the pain was still festering deep inside him. He had said she'd left him for another man, which would no doubt have hurt him deeply, in spite of his laid-back personality. No man liked to be betrayed in such a way. But it still plagued Amelia to think he had only become involved with her to expunge the pain of his past relationship. She could hardly hope to measure up to a woman who moved in the sort of circles Alex did. She'd had nothing to offer him before and now even less so.

'She was crazy to let you go,' she said softly, trailing her fingers down the length of his arm closest her.

'Because of my royal connections?' he asked, turning to face her with a teasing smile, his earlier tension gone.

'You're not supposed to say the *P* word, remember?'

He laughed and pressed her down onto the sand and kissed her soundly before lifting his head to look down at her. 'How about this for another *P* word. Want to come back to my house and play?'

She ran her fingertip over his bottom lip. 'What did you have in mind?'

He drew her finger into his mouth and sucked on it hard, his dark eyes sending her a message that set off a riot of sensation deep and low inside her. 'Do I really need to answer that?' he asked.

'No,' she said as she raised her mouth to meet his. 'You don't.'

A short time later, Alex led her inside his cottage and directed her towards the bathroom. 'You can have the first shower. I have a couple of e-mails to send. I promised my parents I'd keep in close contact with my sister. She's backpacking her way around Europe.'

She gave him a grateful look. 'Thanks. I feel as if I've got sand in places I didn't even know I had places.'

He gave her a sexy smile. 'But don't take too long or I might come in and join you.'

Amelia deliberately took her time to see if he was as good as his promise. She used the fragrant shampoo and conditioner in the shower stall and the shower gel that made her skin silky smooth. She closed her eyes and lifted her face to the shower head, delighting in the luxury of hot water that she hadn't had to heat herself.

Her eyes sprang open when the shower stall door opened and Alex stepped in, his naked body brushing up against hers.

'Any hot water left?' he asked.

She stared at the droplets of water running down his face to his mouth. 'Yes.'

'Want to soap my back for me?'

'Um…all right…'

He turned around and, taking a breath, she ran her hands over his muscled back with the shower gel, her fingers lingering over his taut buttocks.

'How about the front?' he asked.

She swallowed. 'The front?'

He turned around, a twinkle appearing in his dark gaze as it meshed with hers. 'The front.'

She took a handful of shower gel and placed it on his chest, keeping her eyes well away from what was probing insistently against the softness of her belly.

'Lower,' he said, his eyes burning into hers.

She swallowed again, her stomach tripping over itself. 'L-lower?'

'Much lower.'

Her soapy hands went down, pausing over his belly button, her fingertip exploring the tight, hairy cave before her hand went a little farther…

His groan as her fingers brushed against him gave her courage and she did it again, more confident this time, shaping him with increasing boldness.

'Look at me,' he commanded roughly.

'I am looking at you,' she said.

'No,' he said. 'Look at what you're doing to me.'

Another tiny swallow and she looked. He was turgid with

need, a need she could feel building in her own body. Her breasts were tight, her legs watery and her stomach quivering with anticipation.

'Now it's my turn,' he said and spun her around.

She sucked in a ragged breath as he soaped her back in long, sensual strokes, his fingers dipping in between her legs in a tantalising not-quite-where-she-wanted-it-most caress.

He stood so close she could feel the hard probe of his body against her, the satin strength of him reminding her of how her gently upward-slanted body was perfectly designed to accept him.

'Turn around,' he said, his voice sounding deep and uneven.

Amelia slowly turned around, her body brushing against the entire length of his.

Hot liquid fire was blazing in his eyes as they met hers. His hands went to the smooth swell of her breasts, his thumb finding each tight nipple until she could hardly think for the pleasure his touch evoked. He bent his head and suckled on her, his tongue sending arrows of heat to the tender, dark, moist recess of her body that was already pulsing with a drumbeat-like need.

His mouth left her breast to capture her mouth in a drugging kiss that left her feeling as liquid as the water spilling around them. The back of the shower stall supported her, for her legs would not, the pressure of his body against hers the only thing keeping her from sliding to the floor.

Alex lifted his mouth from hers, his eyes sending her a message that was as timeless as it was overwhelmingly tempting.

She drew in a scalding breath and ran her hands over him, less shyly this time, her fingers taking him on a journey of sensuality that surprised her even as it drew the harsh guttural groans from the depths of his throat.

'No,' he groaned, stilling the increasingly rapid movement of her hand. 'I can't take any more.'

She wriggled her fingers in his hand but he refused to let her have access to him, instead holding her hand above her head against the back of the shower as he fed hungrily off her mouth.

She felt herself sagging into him, her body thrumming with a need so consuming she pushed herself against him, her body searching for the heated trajectory of his.

She heard him groan as he surged forward, sheathing himself completely, the liquid silk of her body grabbing at him possessively.

Her head rolled back as he drove forward again, her eyes tightly shut as the sky-rocketing sensations flooded her being. It was wild and wanton, urgent and frantic, leaving no room for thoughts, just feelings. She could feel the delicious pressure building, every nerve in her body climbing higher and higher for the release it craved.

He increased his pace at the same time as he reached between her legs, his long fingers touching her where she needed it most. It triggered the response her body ached for, sending a riot of exploding sensations right throughout her, leaving her weightless and trembling in his tight embrace, the echo of her panting cries filling her ears.

She opened her passion-slaked eyes to see his face contort with pleasure as he surged forward again, once, twice, three times, his whole body shuddering against her with the force of his explosive release. He sagged against her, his head burrowed into her neck, his erratic breathing moving his chest in and out against hers.

Amelia held him close, the water cascading around them mingling with the essence of maleness that had burst from his body and branded her as his in the most intimate way possible.

Alex gave her an apologetic grimace as he eased himself out of her hold. 'I told myself I was going to resist you until we got to the bedroom so I could use a condom. I'm not normally so irresponsible, but I just can't seem to help myself around you.'

'I'm sure it will be all right,' she said. 'My period is due any day now.'

'That's not the point,' he said as he turned off the water. 'Cycles can go out of whack and you could find yourself in a situation you hadn't planned for. I won't let it happen again, I promise.'

He reached for a towel and began drying her, each brush of his hands through the towel making her skin cry out for the touch of his bare flesh on hers.

They were both still wet when they landed on the bed in a tangle of limbs, but it only added to the sensations coursing through Amelia as she fell back amongst the pillows with his weight on top of her.

His kiss was hot and demanding, his obvious impatience the biggest compliment she had ever received. It made her feel womanly, powerful and irresistible.

His mouth was on her breasts, then on her stomach, his tongue anointing the tiny dish of her belly button before going lower. Her breath came to a screeching halt when his warm breath fanned over her sensitive feminine folds, her limbs tightening in both apprehension and anticipation. When he parted her tenderly with his tongue, her whole body shivered with reaction, the overly sensitive nerves fizzing with the electric current of his intimate touch. Her response was too hard to hold back; it came in wave after wave of escalating ecstasy until her mind was empty of everything but the exquisite feelings he triggered in her.

Her breathing was still erratic as he reached across her for a condom, deftly placing it on himself before he moved between her thighs with unmistakable urgency. She felt her body grip him, the silken sheath slippery with her fragrant response to him.

She felt him check himself, as if he was trying to hold back his pace, but she wouldn't allow it, her body wanted him hot, hard, heavy and full speed ahead. She arched her back to bring herself closer to him, her hips undulating with the pleasure of his strong movements, each deep thrust sending a shock wave of feeling through her entire body.

Suddenly she was there again, at that impossibly high altitude of pleasure where thoughts were lost in the moment of utterly fulfilling release. Her whole body shivered with it, every nerve and muscle reacting to the flood of sensation that flowed over her and through her like a tide of warm, bubbly water.

Even as her tension left her body, Amelia felt his tension building as each deep thrust brought him closer to the edge. She felt it in his iron-like hold, she felt it in the hot moistness of his mouth as it fed hungrily off hers, and she felt it in the bunched muscles of his buttocks where her hands were holding on to him like an anchor.

He gave one harsh groan into her mouth as he fell forward, the sudden expulsion of his life force rendering him momentarily powerless. He relaxed under her stroking hands, his chest rising and falling against hers, his sweat-slicked body still intimately joined to hers.

Amelia didn't want to move. Her body felt languorous with the aftermath of his lovemaking, all her limbs feeling weightless, as if the bones had been taken out and marshmallow put in their place.

Alex propped himself up on one elbow and pressed a soft kiss to her mouth. 'I bet you didn't learn any of that in that convent of yours, huh?'

She smiled and stretched like a well-fed cat. 'No, I certainly didn't.'

He brushed a strand of her hair away from her cheek. 'You totally rock me, Amelia, do you know that?'

She lowered her gaze a fraction. 'We're not in love with each other.... I know you'll think it terribly old-fashioned of me, but to me it seems a little wrong to be sharing this level of intimacy when we're not committed emotionally.'

'I don't see anything wrong with exploring the attraction we both feel,' he said.

'But how long will it last without stronger feelings to support it?'

'You never know—you might fall in love with me,' he said with a glinting smile.

'I'm not too sold on rapid emotional responses,' she said with a small, almost undetectable downturn of her mouth. 'They can't really be counted on as the real thing.'

'Ah, such cynicism in one so young,' he lamented playfully.

'I'm not being cynical, I'm being realistic. Flash-in-the-pan emotions are exactly that—one flash and they're gone. It happened that way with my ex-lover. I felt sure I was in love with him, I would have staked my life on it, but in the end those feelings died.'

'Plenty of people develop strong and lasting feelings in a short space of time. My parents are living proof of love at first sight.'

Her face clouded with sadness. 'My mother fell in love with my father and it destroyed her life....'

Alex was still thinking about how to respond when his mobile phone began to ring from the bedside table. He reached across Amelia to pick it up.

'Dr Hunter?' an urgent male voice spoke. 'My name is Rico Vialli. I'm looking for my sister, Amelia. Is she with you?'

'Yes, she is. Do you want to—'

'*Oh, thank God...*' The man's voice broke over the words. 'I thought she was dead too....'

Alex sat up, his hand tightening on the phone as his gaze flicked to Amelia's puzzled one. 'What's wrong?' he asked. 'Has something happened?'

He heard Amelia's brother take an unsteady breath and it seemed an eternity before he spoke, his voice coming out like a hoarse croak as he finally announced, 'Our father died earlier this evening.'

'I'm so very sorry—' Alex began but Rico cut him off.

'You don't understand, Dr Hunter,' he said hollowly. 'My father did not die of lung cancer after all. He was burned to death in the cottage. And I don't think it was an accident.'

CHAPTER FOURTEEN

'WHAT'S wrong?' Amelia got to her feet unsteadily as Alex put the phone down after he finished the call.

He met her worried gaze. 'I'm sorry, Amelia, but I have some terrible news for you.'

'My father's dead?'

Alex wished he could find a way to soften the blow. He sat her down and took her hands in his, gently stroking them as he told her what Rico had told him.

'Murdered?' She gaped at him in horror.

'It appears that way according to what your brother just said. The cottage was completely gutted.'

She pulled out of his hold and got to her feet, reaching for something to cover herself with. 'I can't believe it...' she said as she struggled back into her clothes. 'I was only talking to him this morning.... *Oh, Papà!'* She put her head in her hands.

Alex threw on his bathrobe and came to her and held her close. 'Rico said the police are interviewing the nearest neighbours to see if they heard or saw anything. He borrowed one of their phones to call me. He was worried you might have been in the cottage when it burned down.'

She eased herself away to look up at him. 'Is there nothing left? Nothing at all?'

He shook his head grimly.

She sagged against him. 'I don't know what to do....'

'You can stay with me,' he said. 'The police will no doubt want to speak with you at some point, but there's no need to go up there right away. The forensics team will need to do their investigations.'

'W-where is my father's body?'

'I'm not sure,' he said. 'But I would advise against seeing him.'

'He's my father. I want to say goodbye.'

'I know you do, but do you really want your last memory of him to be tainted by what you'll see if you go there this minute?'

Amelia knew he was right; she'd seen enough burn victims to know how hard it was to cope with seeing their often disfiguring wounds. It was distressing enough dealing with strangers as patients, let alone a full-blood relative.

'Has Silvio been contacted?' she asked.

'Yes, Rico said he was on his way,' Alex said. 'He has taken charge of everything.'

'Is he all right?'

'He's pretty shaken up but then who wouldn't be?'

She moved out of his hold and rubbed at her upper arms in agitation. 'My father was dying—everyone knew that. Who would want to hurry his death in such a way?'

Alex had been thinking the very same thing and so far hadn't come up with any answers. 'I'm not sure. Maybe someone wanted him to keep quiet about his role in my kidnap. When you think about it, he's really the only one who could verify who I am.'

She turned to look at him, her eyes wide with alarm. 'Do you think someone else knows who you are—apart from my brothers and me, I mean?'

He frowned as he thought about it. 'I don't know...possibly.'

'My father is not the only person who could verify your

identity,' she said. 'What about the couple who took you to Australia to be adopted?'

His brows met over his eyes. 'You think they could have something to do with this?'

'My father said it cost him everything to keep things quiet. I can only assume he meant the couple he paid to take you away.'

Alex rubbed at his jaw for a moment, the rasp of his hand against his unshaven skin almost too loud in the silence of the room. 'It would seem feasible they wouldn't want their role in it exposed,' he said. 'If they got wind of your father wanting to confess to his part in it they might have wanted to shut him up in case they were hauled before the courts.'

'The whole island has been talking about you ever since you arrived,' she reminded him. 'News often travels between the ports of Mont Avellana and Sicily. Perhaps the couple heard of it and became worried.'

'The one thing I know is you are best kept out of it, Amelia,' he said with a worried frown. 'Your brothers, too, need to keep their heads down until the police find out who is responsible.'

Amelia felt her stomach drop. 'You think we could be in some sort of danger?'

He gave her a sombre look. 'You're a Vialli. You've told me yourself how you've been a target for taunts. Who knows what people will be incited to do?'

She bit her lip in agitation. 'Maybe you should tell the king who you are right away.'

'I don't really think that's necessary just yet. I think we should stick with the plan to get his surgery over and done with, and once he's on the mend I might come forward.'

'What do you mean you *might* come forward? You *have* to come forward!'

'I came to this island as a commoner and I can just as easily leave as one,' he said.

She frowned at him incredulously. 'You mean not tell anyone?'

He gave an indifferent shrug. 'It would save a lot of heartache for my family if I leave things as they are. They're going to find it very hard to deal with the circumstances surrounding my adoption. My mother will blame herself, so will my father, not to mention my little sister, who has enough issues of her own to deal with.'

'But what about your other family, your biological brother and sisters?' she asked. 'Aren't they entitled to meet you after all these years of suffering? Don't they have the right to get to know you and welcome you into the family you were born into?'

His jaw tightened a fraction. 'I can't be Alessandro Fierezza.'

'You *are* Alessandro Fierezza whether you like it or not.'

He blew out a heavy sigh. 'What did I do to make my life so complicated?'

She moved towards him and grasped him by the hand. 'I know this is hard for you. It's hard for me too. I have to live with the guilt of my father's role in the destruction of your life. Don't make it worse by turning your back on your heritage.'

He gave her a lopsided smile. 'Those nuns did a really good job on you, didn't they?'

'What do you mean?'

He flicked her cheek with one finger in a gentle caress. 'You positively ooze with guilt.'

'I can't help it… I feel as if this is all my fault.'

'You're not responsible, Amelia. You didn't do anything wrong.'

'Other people won't see it that way.'

'I'm not interested in what other people think.'

Amelia sighed as Alex held her close, her thoughts tumbling around her head erratically.

Her father was dead.

It didn't seem real even though she had been preparing herself for this moment for months.

Alex spoke into her hair, his warm breath lifting the soft strands closest to her face. 'Your father wouldn't have suffered, Amelia. You have to comfort yourself with that. He would have died of smoke inhalation, especially with his lungs under-functioning the way they were. Rico said there was no sign of him trying to escape. He was found in bed.'

She suppressed a shudder and looked up at him. 'I should have been there. If I hadn't been out with you I would have heard something and perhaps been able to save him.'

'You are not to blame yourself,' Alex insisted. 'You had a perfect right to go out. Besides, if your father hadn't wanted you to go he would have said so, don't you think?'

'Yes…I guess you're right.' She gave a little sigh as she recalled her conversation with her father that morning before Rico had driven her to work. Her father had seemed pleased to hear she was spending time with the Australian doctor. He had even smiled as she'd bent down to kiss his sallow cheek and told her to have a good time.

She moved out of Alex's embrace to pace the room, her stomach churning as she thought about the future. The very few possessions she owned were lying in ashes in the remains of the cottage along with the body of her father.

'I don't know what to do…' She savaged her bottom lip again. 'This seems so…so…unreal. I feel like I'm on the outside of myself looking in. It's like it's happening to someone else, not me. How can I have lost my father in such a way? I mean, he was dying of cancer.… Every morning for the last month I've walked past his room and leaned against the door to check if he was still breathing. Now he's dead, murdered…'

'Listen, Amelia,' Alex said, taking her by the arms and holding her still in front of him. 'The police will take charge of this. You will be safe with me. I'll organise for you to have some clothes and essentials brought here. No doubt Rico and Silvio will have friends they can bunk down with.'

Her frown deepened as she looked up at him. 'But the police will surely ask a lot of questions. They'll want to know about possible motives and so on. How can we tell them of our suspicions without revealing your identity? Besides, Rico might have already mentioned something about you....'

Alex's expression clouded for a moment. 'It will take a few days for them to conduct their enquiries. Let's hope that's long enough for me to do the king's surgery. After that, if the news comes out about who I am, then so be it.'

There was the sound of a car pulling up outside and Amelia's eyes widened as they met his. 'Is that the police?' she asked in a whisper.

Alex looked through the gap in the curtains and nodded. He quickly dressed and answered the door and showed the two officers into the room where Amelia was standing, her hands in tight knots in front of her trembling body.

Alex stood to one side as the officers asked a series of questions, which Amelia answered as carefully as she could. Every now and again her worried gaze would flick to his, but if the police thought there was anything suspicious in it they didn't let on, although Alex couldn't help noticing the way the more senior officer watched Amelia with an intensity that was rather unsettling. But after he took copious notes and asked a few more questions about her father's affairs, he reiterated his earlier condolences and left soon after with the junior officer close behind.

Alex closed the door on their exit, his eyes meeting Amelia's across the room. 'I think our secret is safe for the time being but I suspect it won't be long before they put two and two together.'

'I know....' She hugged her arms close to her body. 'I felt like a criminal the whole time they were talking to me. I always do around the police… It's because of my name.' She eased herself away to look up at him. 'I need to see Rico and Silvio just to make sure they're all right. Would you mind if I borrowed your car?'

'Don't be silly,' he said, searching for his keys. 'I'll drive you myself. Do you think they'll still be up there?'

She gave him a weary look as she followed him out to his car. 'They'll be there.'

The thin curl of smoke rising eerily in the night air sent an icy chill down Amelia's spine as Alex drove up the uneven driveway. She stared at the remains of her family home, unable to get her head around the fact that there was nothing left. Not a single photo or article of clothing. There was nothing but the grotesquely charred skeleton of the cottage and silver ashes and the lingering smell of acrid smoke.

Once the last police vehicle drove away Rico and Silvio came over to where she and Alex were standing, their faces white with shock and their bodies visibly shaking as they each in turn enveloped her in a short, somewhat awkward hug.

Rico held out his hand to Alex. 'My father told me who you are,' he said with obvious embarrassment. 'I don't know what to say.…'

Alex shook his hand. 'Your father did what he thought was best at the time. It could have been much worse.'

Rico seemed at a loss for words and looked to his younger brother for help. Silvio shifted uncomfortably and, with a slight hesitation, offered his hand as well. 'I can see the likeness even though it's dark up here,' he said. 'I was the one who first alerted my father to the rumours about you. Does the king know?'

Alex shook his head and explained his reasons for keeping his identity quiet until the king was out of danger.

'Did either of you mention anything to the police about the rumours?' Amelia put in.

'No,' Silvio said. 'I don't even think the police are going to treat this as a murder investigation.'

She stared at him in shock. 'But why not?'

He gave a cynical shrug. 'One less Vialli on the island,' he said. 'There are plenty of people who have always suspected *Papà* was involved with the bandits. They'll be celebrating his death, not grieving it.'

'Has *Papà*…been taken away?' she asked.

'He was taken away a short time ago,' Rico said, swallowing convulsively as he glanced back at the remains of the cottage.

Amelia felt her insides cave in at what her older brother must have come upon when he'd returned to the cottage that evening.

'I was worried you were in there with him,' he said, and took a cigarette from Silvio with a distinct tremble of his hand.

She watched as Silvio flicked his lighter to ignite his brother's cigarette, the sudden flare of light illuminating the shocked pallor of his and Rico's faces, but for once she decided against lecturing them both on the dangers of smoking.

'Have the police found out anything?' she asked instead.

Silvio lit his own cigarette and took a deep drag before answering. 'Apparently no one in the neighbourhood heard or saw anything, or if they did they're not saying. But Rico's right—no doubt the police will make some token enquiries, but this is one case they won't be in a hurry to solve.'

Amelia felt her body begin to shake with reaction. The night was warm, but she began to shiver uncontrollably until Alex drew her close.

'I've arranged for your sister to stay with me for the time being,' he informed Rico and Silvio. 'Do you both have somewhere to stay?'

'Yes,' Silvio answered. 'I have some friends down at the port who will put us both up. I've been staying with them for the last couple of weeks.'

'I'm not planning on staying around once my father's

funeral is over,' Rico stated. 'I want to get away and start a new life without the past getting in the way.'

'Me too,' Silvio said. 'I have work lined up on Mont Avellana. You should think about leaving too, Amelia. Once the news breaks about Dr Hunter's identity it could get really unpleasant for you. Don't forget that whoever is responsible for *Papà*'s death was probably hoping you were in the cottage with him as you have been most nights.'

Amelia swallowed the lump of fear clogging her throat. 'I'm not going to run away,' she said with a determined lift of her chin. 'I have work to do here.'

'I'll keep an eye on her,' Alex assured them. 'She'll be safe with me.'

Physically maybe, but not emotionally, Amelia ruminated sadly as they left a short time later. She sat silently in the car beside Alex as he drove away from the ghostly remains of her family home, her grief over her father taking a second place to the sense of loss she felt at the thought of never being able to tell Alex how much she loved him. Once the news broke of his true identity their relationship would have to end.

Their two worlds had briefly collided but could never stay connected, not unless he was prepared to walk away from everything that was rightfully his, from everything her father had taken away from him thirty-four years ago....

CHAPTER FIFTEEN

ONCE they were back at his cottage, Alex handed Amelia a small tumbler of brandy, his expression still full of concern. 'How are you holding up? This must be such a terrible shock for you.'

She took the brandy and cupped it in her hands. 'It is…. I feel sort of numb.'

'That's understandable. Even when a death is expected it's still a shock when it finally happens, but in this instance it's much harder to deal with, given the circumstances.'

Amelia took a tiny sip of the fiery liquid. 'I know this sounds a bit strange, but I can't help feeling relieved he didn't suffer in the end. Dying from a terminal illness can be so…so awful for the patient as well as the relatives.'

Alex took one of her hands in his and began to stroke it soothingly. 'I know what you mean. I've seen too many people die from lung cancer to be under any illusions of how diffi-cult it is in the last stages.'

Amelia looked at their joined hands before raising her gaze to meet his. 'Alex…it's very kind of you to offer to have me stay here with you, but I feel uncomfortable about what people will say, especially once the news breaks about your identity.'

'They can say what they like,' he said. 'They don't have to know our private arrangements. For all they know you could be sleeping in the spare room just like any other house guest.'

'Maybe I should do that.' She chanced a quick glance at him. 'Sleep in the spare room, I mean.'

He gave her a studied look. 'Is that what you'd prefer?'

She forced herself to hold his unwavering gaze. 'I'm not cut out for this…er…arrangement, as you call it.'

'You want to end our relationship?' he asked.

'I've known from the first that I'm being used to fill in the time,' she said.

His frown brought his dark brows together. 'You think that's what this is about?'

'Isn't it?'

'Of course it isn't. Look, I admit I've fast-tracked our relationship a bit, but that doesn't mean I'm not genuinely attracted to you.'

'But for how long?'

'How can anyone answer that?' he asked. 'I spent two years of my life with a woman I thought was in love with me but she apparently changed her feelings overnight. I'm sorry, Amelia, but I don't feel like making myself that vulnerable again. If you're not happy with our relationship as it stands, then feel free to walk away.'

Amelia inwardly cringed at his words. How could their relationship be genuine when he had no intention of it continuing? He was content to flirt and have fun, but it wasn't for ever. She had been a silly fool to even think for a moment that things could be any different.

'So what you want from me is a no-strings-and-no-emotions-involved temporary sexual relationship?' she asked.

'I hate to drag you kicking and screaming out of the Dark Ages, but being in love with a sexual partner is no longer a prerequisite,' he said. 'People nowadays can have very satisfactory relationships without the complications of feelings that rarely last the distance anyway.'

'So I'm a sex buddy—isn't that what it's called these days?'

'This is not the time for this discussion. You've just lost your father in terrible circumstances. Your whole world is crumbling around you. You need time to get your head around all this and quite frankly so do I.'

Amelia watched as he moved across the room, his back turned towards her. He was right, she thought. This wasn't just about her; it was about him as well. In some ways he had received an even bigger shock than she had. His whole life had changed and he was still trying to negotiate his way through it. She had at least been well prepared for the news of her father's death, and even though it had happened, as Alex had described, under terrible circumstances, at least she was still who she had always been—Amelia Vialli. Alex, on the other hand, had suddenly found himself caught between two worlds: that of his life back in Australia as Dr Alex Hunter surrounded by his loving adoptive family, and his new one here on Niroli, as Prince Alessandro Fierezza with a role set before him that was as daunting as it was inescapable.

But even so it was painful to accept that what they had experienced together was coming to its inevitable end. It had to. She was part of the family that had taken his heritage away from him.

'You're right,' she said, releasing a little sigh. 'This is hard for both of us.'

He turned to look at her. 'It's going to get harder, Amelia. I have to make some decisions in the next few days that less than one per cent of the population ever has to make. Whatever I decide is going to hurt someone somewhere and I'll have to live with that for the rest of my life.'

She swallowed at the anguish she could see written in stark lines on his face. She knew she too was going to be one of the people most likely to be hurt by whatever decision he made. 'I wish I could help you,' she said.

He gave her a twisted smile. 'No one can help me. I have

to do this alone. But right now you are the one who needs support. The next few days are going to be tough on you.'

'I'll be fine,' she said, knowing it was a lie. Inside she felt shell-shocked and vulnerable in a way she hadn't felt since her mother had died. She ached to feel secure, but it was as if her whole world were tipping out of control. Alex was offering her his support, but she knew it could only be temporary. He'd made it perfectly clear his emotions were not involved, which she could only assume meant he only saw their relationship as a brief interlude before he made his final decision about his future. The most painful part was recognising that, no matter what he decided, there was no place for her in either choice he made.

The day of the funeral was one of the most miserable days of Amelia's life. For a start it rained constantly, which meant the very few people who were considering attending decided against doing so at the last minute. Even Alex was unable to offer his support when a difficult case went overtime in Theatre.

Her brothers stood stiffly beside her during the brief service, their faces largely impassive, but inside she knew they were feeling the loss as keenly as she was.

Alex showed up just as they were leaving the cemetery and respectfully stood to one side as she said goodbye to her brothers, who were leaving the island the following day.

She joined him a few moments later, her face looking pinched and white, but even so she managed a small smile for him when he took her arm.

'Are you all right?' he asked.

She nodded and let out a little sigh and looked back at the grave that marked her father's final resting place. 'He lived such a hard life, but I can't help feeling he's finally at peace.' She turned back to look at him. 'How did your case go?'

'It was touch and go there for a while, but we managed to pull a miracle out of the hat. Sorry I couldn't make it in time.'

'It's all right,' she said as she let down her umbrella now the rain had ceased. 'You of all people wouldn't be expected to pay your last respects.'

He let a small silence fill the space between them before he announced, 'I'm doing the surgery on the king first thing tomorrow.'

Her throat moved up and down as she held his gaze. 'Are you nervous?'

'Why should I be?' he asked. 'As far as I'm concerned he's just like any other patient.'

'But he's not just any other patient. He's—'

Alex placed the pad of his index finger against her lips to silence her. 'As far as I'm concerned he's just an old man in need of bypass surgery.'

Amelia felt her lips tingling at his touch, brief as it was. She felt as if she couldn't get enough of his touch even though she had spent every night since her father's death in Alex's arms. She knew their relationship was on borrowed time; the sense of urgency she felt had taken their intimacy to increasingly erotic levels until her whole body felt as if it would never be the same. She longed to tell him she loved him but knew it would not achieve anything except further pain for her in the end.

'I have to get back to the hospital,' Alex said with a quick glance at his watch. 'Are you working at the palace tonight?'

She nodded. 'But don't worry, I can make my own way there. Rico has left me the car.'

'I guess I'll see you at the hospital tomorrow afternoon.'

'Yes,' she said, forcing her lips into a tight smile. 'Good luck in the morning. I hope it goes well.'

His expression clouded for a brief moment. 'Yeah… thanks. I hope it does too.'

She watched him walk back towards his car, his long strides taking him farther and farther away. She could feel the words to call him back tightening her throat, but they couldn't get past the knot of emotion lodged there.

'I'm so sorry about your father,' Lucia said the following afternoon when Amelia came on the ward. 'Are you all right?'

'I'm fine,' Amelia said as she put her bag away. 'It was a horrible shock, but I'm coming to terms with it…more or less.'

'Have the police found out what happened?'

'The case is now closed,' she said with a despondent sigh. 'I was speaking to them before I came on duty. They're putting it down to an accident, apparently suggesting my father fell asleep while he was smoking in bed.'

Lucia grimaced in empathy. 'That's exactly what happened to my grandmother. She'd been told a thousand times not to smoke in bed, but she wouldn't listen. Fortunately she woke up before things got out of control, but the very next week she was back at it, much to my mother's disgust.'

Amelia met Lucia's gaze. 'My father gave up smoking as soon as he found out he had cancer.'

Lucia's eyes went wide. 'What are you saying?'

'I don't know. He could have fallen asleep with a candle burning, but I can't help feeling uneasy about it all.'

'You mean you think it wasn't an accident? That he was…' she swallowed over the word '…murdered?'

'I don't know. The police don't think so, but there are certainly people on the island who would have liked to see him dead.'

'Has this got something to do with Alex Hunter?' Lucia asked.

Amelia tried to disguise her startled look. 'What makes you say that?'

'I don't know. It's just when my mother came over to help me with the girls she told me how everyone is talking about Alex Hunter's amazing likeness to the Fierezzas and how people are speculating on whether the prince was actually killed all those years ago. I suppose you've heard the rumours? They think Alex Hunter is Prince Alessandro.' Lucia gave a little chuckle of disbelief. 'It's totally crazy, don't you think? If you ask me, I think it shows just how old and desperate the king has become in looking for an heir to take his place.'

'Yes…it's certainly crazy…'

Lucia gave her a probing look. '*You're* not starting to believe all that nonsense, are you?'

Amelia avoided the other woman's eyes as she tidied some papers on the desk. 'If the palace officials think Alex Hunter is the prince, then surely they will conduct their own investigations to prove it either way.'

'Have you heard how the king's surgery went?' Lucia asked, glancing at the clock on the wall. 'It should be over by now.'

'No, not yet, but no news is good news, I suppose.'

'Were you on at the palace last night? How did the king seem?'

'He didn't sleep very well,' Amelia answered. 'But I guess that was to be expected. It's a big operation for an elderly man.'

She didn't tell her friend about the general air of excitement she'd been able to feel the whole time she had been there. The castle staff had bustled about in an atmosphere of high expectation, which she felt sure had nothing to do with the king's surgery. She wondered how they had come to know of Alex's identity. Had her father spoken to someone before he had died or had the palace staff activated their own investigation?

As she'd left the palace that morning she had wandered past the tiny grave of the child who had been buried in place of the prince, but there had been no fresh flowers in the brass vase, which had seemed to her to be rather remiss. It was as if the little child was to be of no significance now the real prince had been located.

'Poor little baby,' she'd murmured softly as she'd bent down to empty the sour water from the vase and replace the faded blooms with some sweet-smelling roses that had been growing nearby.

Lucia broke through her thoughts. 'At least the king is in the very best of hands,' she said, and then added with a teasing smile, 'and, speaking of those very clever hands, have they been anywhere near you lately? I heard you're sharing his cottage. Could it be you're sharing his bed as well?'

Amelia could feel her face heating, but forced herself to meet the other woman's gaze. 'Alex Hunter isn't going to be here for much longer. I would be a fool to get involved with him in anything other than a temporary way.'

Lucia's eyes twinkled as she leaned closer conspiratorially. 'But you're tempted, aren't you? Go on, admit it. He's totally irresistible. If I wasn't married with two kids and in desperate need of a tummy tuck, I'd make a play for him myself.'

Amelia was relieved when a patient pressed the buzzer by his bedside for attention. She gave Lucia a weak smile and headed off down the corridor, but she felt her friend's speculative gaze following her all the way.

Amelia had not long finished attending to the patient who had summoned her when she caught sight of Alex coming down the corridor to the cardiac unit with Dr Morani by his side.

'Ah, Amelia,' the doctor greeted her cheerily. 'We've just returned from the private hospital. We have wonderful news. The king has come through the surgery very well. He is expected to make a full recovery. Alex did a brilliant job.'

'Congratulations,' she addressed Alex, not surprised at how tired he looked. 'It must be a relief to have it over with.'

He let out a barely audible sigh. 'It is.'

'Dr Hunter?' The cardiac unit ward clerk came towards them with a harried look on her face. 'There are some royal officials waiting to speak to you in your office. They refused to make an appointment and insisted on waiting.'

Alex met Amelia's eyes briefly before turning back to the ward clerk. 'It's all right. I'll see them now. I can do a round later.' He looked at Dr Morani and asked, 'You don't mind if Sister Vialli comes with me, do you, Vincenzo?'

'Of course not,' Dr Morani replied. 'Things are pretty quiet on the ward.'

Amelia blinked at Alex once the others had moved on. 'Me?'

'Yes, you,' Alex said, leading her by the elbow towards his office.

'Do you think this is about you know what?' she asked in a worried undertone.

His expression was grim as he glanced down at her. 'It looks like it,' he said. 'Just before I scrubbed for his operation the king grasped my arm before being anaesthetised. He looked at my birthmark scars for a moment and then looked me in the eye and called me Alessandro with tears in his eyes. I had a hard time keeping my head throughout the procedure, especially as the theatre staff were giving me speculative looks all the time.'

'But you did it, Alex,' she said softly. 'The operation was a success.'

He didn't answer, but opened his office door and indicated for her to go in before him, but Amelia could tell he was struggling to deal with the situation now it was coming to a head.

Four men in suits stood as they came into the room, their expressions speaking for them as their collective gaze went to Alex.

Amelia stood silently as the leader stepped forward and informed Alex of the investigations that had been conducted over his identity, including the details of his adoption. They had even gone so far as to apply for a warrant to examine his medical records, which clearly documented the removal of a strawberry birthmark several years ago. They had also gone to the extraordinary lengths of conducting a DNA test on the glass he had sipped from on the first night he had gone to the palace.

'So there's absolutely no doubt?' Alex asked once the man finished.

The official shook his head. 'No doubt at all. You are His Royal Highness Prince Alessandro Fierezza. Your family will want to spend time with you as soon as the king is out of hospital and a press release has already been prepared to be released immediately.'

Alex visibly stiffened. 'I'd like this kept out of the press for as long as possible. I would like some time to prepare my adoptive family of this news. It will come as a dreadful shock to them.'

'We will do what we can, but I can make no promises,' the official said. 'The king gave instructions that as soon as your identity was verified a press statement would be released.'

Amelia saw Alex's throat move up and down and her heart tightened painfully at what he must be going through.

'We have made arrangements for you to move into the royal household immediately,' the official said.

'No.' Alex held up his hand. 'I need some time to get used to this. I'd prefer my own private space for the time being.'

'But King Giorgio will be concerned for your safety,' the official insisted. 'And you will need to be briefed on your royal duties.'

'I don't care,' Alex said implacably. 'I still have work to do and I don't see any reason to change my living arrangements.'

'Your work will have to end,' the official said. 'The king will not allow you to maintain your profession. It is against royal protocol. The ruler of Niroli must devote his life to the kingdom. Therefore maintaining a profession is out of the question.'

Alex's jaw tightened, but he didn't answer, Amelia assumed because he didn't trust himself to remain polite. She could see the tension move from his jaw to encompass his whole body; even his spine was rigid with it and his expression dark as a stormy cloud.

'There is one other rather sensitive subject we wish to bring up with you.' The leading official spoke into the stiff silence. 'But perhaps it would be best if the young lady was not present when we discuss it.'

Amelia felt her face begin to flame, but as she made a move to leave Alex's strong fingers captured her wrist and brought her back to his side. 'No,' he said. 'I would prefer for her to stay.'

'Very well.' The official looked distinctly uncomfortable. 'It has come to the king's attention that you are currently…er…involved in a relationship with Miss Vialli. Is that correct?'

'I don't see that it's anyone's business but my own,' Alex responded coolly.

'It is everybody's business when the woman you have chosen to be involved with is the daughter of the man who kidnapped you when you were an infant. The people of Niroli will not accept her, not even as your mistress.'

'Amelia had nothing to do with her father's activities,' Alex pointed out. 'I don't see why she should be discriminated against for something she had nothing whatsoever to do with.'

'Are you saying that your current relationship with Miss Vialli is likely to become more permanent?'

Amelia held her breath as she waited for Alex to respond to the official's blunt question. The silence stretched and stretched like a thin wire that at any moment could snap and flick back with a stinging blow.

'My relationship with Miss Vialli is not something I am prepared to discuss right now,' Alex finally said. 'Now if you'll excuse me, I have patients to see.'

'We will be in contact with you tomorrow,' one of the other officials informed him. 'There are legal matters to see to and you will need to be advised on official protocol and your schedule of duties. Also, your siblings will want to speak with you.'

'Thank you for your time,' the leading official said. 'We realise this is a very difficult situation for you and the king will not want you to suffer any undue stress.'

'Thanks, I really appreciate it,' Alex said, with no attempt to tone down his sarcasm.

One of the men turned to face Amelia just as they were leaving. 'The king has advised me to terminate your contract at the palace. He will no longer need your services as a nurse,' he informed her officiously before turning with the others to leave.

Amelia waited until the door had closed on their exit before she brought her gaze to meet Alex's. 'You really didn't have to spare my feelings, Alex,' she said with a distinct chill in her tone. 'You could have told them straight out that our relationship wasn't permanent.'

He frowned darkly. 'I'm not prepared to be told how to live my life, certainly not at my age.'

'But it's true what they said. I won't be accepted as your mistress. They don't even want me to take care of the king any more.' She took an unsteady breath and continued, hoping he wouldn't be able to see through her emotionally detached act. 'I think it's time to say goodbye, Alex. It's not as if we have any lasting feelings for each other. It was nice while it lasted and I really appreciate what you did for me in stepping into the breach after my father died. But I think it's time we ended this relationship. It's not what I want and, if you're honest with yourself, it's not what you want either.'

His mouth was white-tipped as he looked down at her. 'You seem to have made up your mind about this. Is there any point in me trying to convince you otherwise?'

'What would be the point?' she asked. 'You have responsibilities to face now that people know who you are. Like my brothers, I no longer want to live my life in the shadow of what my father did. If I remain involved with you, even temporarily, it will cause further shame and hurt for me and I just can't face it.' She stepped towards him and offered him her hand. 'Goodbye, Alex.'

He took her hand and held it for longer than necessary. 'Where will you stay?' he asked, his fingers intertwining with hers.

She hoped he couldn't see the glimmer of tears in her eyes as she raised her gaze to his. 'Signora Gravano is planning to visit her daughter. I will probably house-sit for her until I decide what to do.'

He gave her a ghost of a smile. 'If ever you need to take the short cut I'll make sure that bramble is under control.'

She smiled at his attempt at his old humour. 'I won't be taking any short cuts any more. I think I might too move on once I get a bit of money behind me.'

His eyes were dark and serious as they held hers. 'If you need anything I'd be happy to help. Money or whatever, you only have to ask.'

Amelia adopted a flippant tone for the sake of her pride. 'I guess I could always get a personal reference from you. Now that would look good on my CV. I'd be able to get any job I wanted.'

A small frown began to wrinkle his brow. 'The press will no doubt start hounding you. Can I trust you to keep our previous relationship out of the newspapers?'

It hurt her that he even had to ask, but she did her best not to show it. 'What happened between us was a little fling that has no relevance to anyone but us.' She gave him a fabricated smile and hoped it would pass for the real thing. 'I bet you won't even remember what my name was in a year's time, Alex—or should I call you Prince Alessandro?'

His eyes fell away from hers as he released her hand. 'Right at this moment, little elf, I don't know who the hell I am.'

'You'll always be Alex Hunter to me,' she said softly, but she wasn't sure if he'd even heard her. He had moved to stand in front of the window, his eyes looking out to the distance, his back turned towards hers, his shoulders looking as if the weight of the whole new world he was about to face were pressing down on them.

CHAPTER SIXTEEN

'OF COURSE you can stay with me,' Signora Gravano said as she ushered Amelia inside her cottage. 'So it's true then? Dr Hunter is actually the prince?'

'Yes, it's true,' Amelia said, letting her small bag drop to the floor with a sad little thud. 'He is the prince.'

'The poor man.' Signora Gravano sighed. 'Think of what he must be going through.'

'I know,' she said with a sigh. 'I can't help thinking about his adoptive family as well. This sort of thing affects everyone.'

'I know it must be hard for you too, Amelia, but you surely can't have been thinking there was a future in your relationship with him, especially once you knew who he really was?'

Amelia sank to the nearest chair and put her head in her hands. 'I know…but a girl can always dream, can't she?'

The old woman stroked the black silk of Amelia's hair. 'I feel sorry for both of you. You have both been caught between two very different worlds. He has responsibilities he must face now that he has discovered his birth origins.'

'I just wish I could have had more time with him.'

'He is a member of a royal family, my dear. You have to accept that.'

Amelia lifted her reddened eyes to the old woman's. 'I know…it's just hard to fall in love with someone and then they suddenly turn into someone else…someone unreachable… unattainable…'

'You poor child—so you have truly fallen in love with him?'

She nodded miserably. 'I just couldn't help it.'

'What about his feelings?'

'He's not in love with me,' she said miserably. 'He just wanted a quick fling and, fool that I am, I agreed to it.'

'How has he coped with the news of his past? It must have come as a complete shock to find he is a prince.'

Amelia thought about it for a moment. 'He's definitely changed. When I first met him he was so funny…so light-hearted and easygoing. I really liked that about him. But since he found out about his past he's become…I don't know…sort of different…serious, and he hardly smiles any more.'

'It is a highly unusual set of circumstances,' the old woman pointed out. 'Most people who go in search of their birth parents worry they might uncover some sort of abuse or criminal behaviour in their family of origin. Instead, Dr Hunter has found out he is heir to a throne, not to mention the details of his kidnap as an infant.'

'Which my father was responsible for,' Amelia reminded her unnecessarily.

'Yes, that makes it all the more difficult, but if he had genuine feelings for you he would not let something like that stand in his way.'

Amelia let out a heavy sigh. She had been thinking the very same thing. If Alex Hunter wanted her in his life on a permanent basis wouldn't he have said so by now?

'He doesn't have genuine feelings for me. Right from the start I've known he's been here for a good time, not a long time. Even now that he's found out who he really is doesn't change that. If he decides to stay and take up the throne there would be no way he would be able to have me as his partner. The king has already dismissed me as his nurse and Alex stood there and said nothing in my defence as the officials delivered the news. But even if he did choose to return to his life in Australia and took me with him, how could his adoptive parents ever accept me given my background and my father's role in his kidnap?'

Signora Gravano gave her a sympathetic look. 'It seems you are not unlike your dear mother after all, Amelia. You fell in love with the wrong man at the wrong time.'

Amelia felt the weighty truth of her elderly friend's words like a burdensome yoke around her neck. Her mother's dreams of a happy, settled life with the man she loved so desperately had been totally shattered by circumstances beyond her control. And now Amelia's life was heading along the same pathway to destruction, there seemed no way of avoiding similar heartbreak. She loved a man whom she could not have, a man who did not want her, and—even if he did—would have to give up everything in order to have her.

Amelia was glad her part-time shifts at the community health centre kept her away from the Free Hospital for the next couple of days. The thought of running into Alex in the hospital corridors or on the ward was far too upsetting. She still couldn't quite believe she had managed to convince him she was no longer interested in him. She had secretly hoped he would have put up more of a fight, but he had taken her rejection with barely a flinch of male pride.

She had heard that the king was now back at the palace, having made an excellent recovery from his surgery and, as expected, the press had gone wild with the news of Alex Hunter's true identity. For the most part she had tried to ignore the news reports and papers, but it was impossible to escape the sense of excitement filling the island at the news of the prince's return to his rightful home.

Late one afternoon Amelia ran into Lucia as she was doing a last-minute errand for an elderly patient.

'Amelia, I'm so glad I caught you. There's been a journalist hanging out at the hospital for days desperate to speak to you.'

'They want to speak to *me*?' Amelia blinked at her friend in shock.

'Of course they want to speak to you,' Lucia answered. 'It's exactly what the big-name magazines are looking for, the interview with the prince's recent love interest. You could make an absolute fortune out of it.'

Amelia's heart began to thud in alarm. 'You didn't tell them anything, did you?'

Lucia looked a little shamefaced. 'Well…er…not much.'

Amelia gave her a penetrating look. 'How much?'

Lucia bit her lip. 'I'm sorry…but the journalist was so persistent and since you don't have a phone…I sort of told them what I knew.'

Amelia closed her eyes as she pinched the bridge of her nose in distress. 'Oh, Lucia, how could you?'

'I'm sorry. I just thought since it was all over between you now you wouldn't mind. It's not like you're seeing him any more. He's up at the palace being briefed on what's expected of him now he's finished his work at the hospital.'

So that was why she hadn't seen any sign of him at the cottage, Amelia thought as she chewed the rough end of one nail.

'I'm sure it won't do much harm for people to know you and Prince Alessandro were an item,' Lucia said. 'The journalist was intrigued with the whole Vialli bandit thing. It gave it that whole star-crossed lovers angle.'

'I'll have to see Alex and explain it wasn't me,' Amelia said, beginning to gnaw at her bottom lip instead of her nail.

'Why shouldn't you cash in on this, Amelia?' Lucia asked. 'It's not as if this won't happen again. Any woman he looks at in the future will be instant newspaper fodder. You might as well get something out of it while you can. The way I see it, he used you. He had his little fling, but as soon as he found out who he really was he let you go.'

Amelia didn't bother telling Lucia it was her who had been the one to put an end to their relationship. 'Has the article been printed yet?' she asked.

'It came out this morning,' Lucia said, and, rummaging in her bag, handed her a glossy magazine. 'It's on page three.'

Amelia opened the magazine and grimaced as she saw a photo of Alex and her sitting at the restaurant in Santa Fiera on their first date. 'How on earth did they get this photo?' she asked.

'Someone must have taken it in the restaurant and sold it to the magazine,' Lucia suggested.

Amelia quickly read through the article and closed the magazine with trembling fingers. 'Oh, Lucia, it makes me sound like a social-climbing tart using him to make myself a fortune.'

'Yes…well, the journalist did stretch the truth a bit, I thought,' Lucia said with another sheepish look as she took the magazine back and stuffed it in her bag.

Amelia let out her breath in a ragged stream. 'He asked me not to speak to anyone about our relationship. I'll have to see him and apologise.'

'I don't like your chances,' Lucia said. 'He's a prince now, remember? You can't just turn up and see him or even make an appointment. Any contact you have has to be approved by the palace officials.'

Amelia knew she wasn't going to be welcome at the palace, but she had to see Alex again regardless. She made her way there as soon as she could, but, as she had more or less expected, the guards refused her entry. She pleaded with them, but they remained coldly resolute until Alex appeared from around a corner.

'It's all right, gentlemen,' he said. 'Miss Vialli will not be here for long.'

Amelia felt the bite of Alex's fingers as he practically dragged her into one of the side doors of the ancient palace by one arm. 'Just the person I want to see,' he said, closing the door behind them.

She tried to pull out of his hold but his fingers tightened. 'I should have known you weren't to be trusted,' he ground out. 'How much did they pay you for that interview?'

'I didn't give an interview—' she began, but he cut her off.

'You probably knew all along who I was. No doubt your family put you up to this. You're a Vialli, after all. Treachery is in your blood. You saw a chance to make a fortune out of this and you went for it the first chance you could.'

'No…that's not true, Alex—'

'Don't insult me by lying to me now you've achieved what you set out to achieve,' he lambasted her. 'You lied to me from the start. No doubt that little convent story was part of the whole attempt to lure me in. But you're no innocent. You're a scheming little traitor like the rest of your family. I feel disgusted with myself for falling for it. You were simply waiting until you could get what you wanted out of it.'

'No—' Her one-word denial came out strangled, but he carried on as if she hadn't spoken.

'I even fancied myself in love with you for a time, but that was all part of your plan, wasn't it?' he asked coldly. 'To get me to the point where I had to choose between you and the throne. I can't have both and you knew it. What a victory that would have been for your republican family. The kidnapped heir was finally returned, but he was as good as useless as he wanted the very thing that would take away his right to the kingdom.'

'No,' she began again, her stomach churning in despair. 'You don't understand…'

His eyes blazed like black diamonds as they hit on hers. 'You've wasted your efforts, Amelia. I don't want you or the throne,' he said. 'I've made up my mind. I'm going back to Australia to continue my work. I've already told the king.'

Amelia moistened her dry mouth as she struggled to take in what he'd said.

He dragged a hand through his hair and continued, 'They're not happy, of course, but I have to do what is right for me. My real family is the one who reared me and loved me for the last thirty-four years. I had nothing to do with what happened in the past. It was a quirk of fate, and I don't see why I should give up years of intensive training to take on a role I have no desire for. I might be a prince by birthright, but that's not who I am now.'

She stared at him speechlessly, her emotions in complete turmoil. He was turning down his right to the throne, but for all the wrong reasons. It had nothing to do with her. She would never have stood in his way, even though it would have cost her everything.

'Aren't you going to say anything in your defence?' he asked. 'Haven't you got some carefully prepared speech to convince me of your innocence? That's what I would expect from someone like you.'

Amelia met his glittering gaze. 'I can't change your mind, Alex. You've come to the decisions you'd made on the basis of what you believe to be true and no doubt anything I say will not change your views. I didn't know you were a prince. In fact I didn't even know who you were the first time I met you. You could have been a peasant just like me rather than the esteemed surgeon you are, but I loved your quirky sense of humour and the way you laughed at life.'

Alex watched as she brushed a tear from the corner of her eye, but he didn't reach out to her.

'I feel sad that you no longer have that ability,' she went on in a soft, regretful tone. 'You've changed since you've found out about your birth origins. I liked the old Alex

much more than the new one, but I guess that's what life
has dished up to you. You are not one person now, but two,
and, as you said, you've had to decide which one you will
be from now on. I admire your decision to be Alex Hunter
the cardiac surgeon, for I think he is the real you, not the
Prince of Niroli.'

Alex swallowed, trying to get control of his emotions.
Could he have got it wrong about her? The palace officials
had hinted at her younger brother's involvement in a second-
wave rebellion against the monarchy, warning him of the
danger of trusting anyone from within the Vialli family.

'I'm sorry about the article you saw,' Amelia said into the
silence. 'I know you won't believe me but I had nothing whatsoever to do with it. I have been working at the community
health centre for the last two days. I haven't been in contact
with any journalists, but unfortunately one of my colleagues
at the Free Hospital took it upon herself to speak for me to a
journalist. I am sorry you have been hurt by that disclosure.
She meant no harm, so please don't hold it against her.'

Alex watched in silence as she moved past him to leave.
He didn't stop her even though he wanted to. The door closed
behind her and he was left with the faint scent of her presence
like a ghost coming back to haunt him.

The pastel fingertips of dawn were streaking the sky when
Amelia returned to the palace the following morning on a
completely different mission. She had determined she would
pay her respects to the innocent little boy whom nobody
seemed to be considering now the real prince had been found.
She had gathered some wildflowers, the early-morning dew
still clinging to their delicate petals like crystal tears.

Fortunately one of the guards on duty recognised her from
the previous day and allowed her through. She thanked him
and moved like a shadow towards the family graveyard only

to come up short when she saw a tall figure standing there looking down at the tiny headstone.

Alex looked up at the sound of her footfall, his expression looking pale, as if he hadn't slept well. His lips moved in the semblance of a rueful smile. 'I thought for a moment you were a ghost.'

She gave him a wry look. 'I would have thought that should have been my line.'

His forehead creased into a frown as he turned back to look at the tiny grave in front of him. 'It's weird looking down at this little grave thinking it could have been me.'

She came to stand next to him, bending down after a moment to carefully arrange the flowers she had brought.

Alex shifted his gaze to the two larger graves with his biological parents' names written above the family motto, an aching poignancy filling his chest that they would for ever remain strangers to him.

'I thought I should do this one last time, but I wonder if anyone will tend to this little boy's grave now,' Amelia said as she straightened and dusted off her hands. 'Maybe they'll dig it up and remove it. After all, he's not the real prince, just a little peasant boy of no significance.'

'Amelia…'

She turned to face him, her spine stiff with what little pride she had left. 'As soon as I have some money I will reimburse you for the items you bought for me after my father's death. It may take a little longer than expected since, as you know, your grandfather no longer requires my services, but I will make sure I get it to you as soon as possible.'

He drew his brows together in a heavy frown. 'He shouldn't have fired you like that,' he said. 'The least he could have done was to tell you to your face instead of sending his officials to do it for him.'

'I didn't hear you offer a word of protest at the time,' she pointed out a little tightly. 'But then perhaps you'd already decided I wasn't to be trusted and was best removed from your life.'

He looked back at the graves once more, his shoulders hunched as he shoved his hands in the pockets of his trousers. 'I shouldn't have accused you of going to the press without checking the facts first.'

'Oh, so someone verified my story, did they? What a pity you didn't believe me in the first place.'

'I don't blame you for being angry with me,' he said, bringing his gaze back to hers. 'I wasn't thinking when I said those things to you last night. I was looking for a scapegoat. Unfortunately my parents had heard the news before I could speak to them personally. It totally devastated them and I'm afraid I took it out on you.'

Amelia's expression softened in concern. 'Are they all right?' she asked. 'What about your sister? Has she heard?'

He gave her a glimmer of a sad smile. 'Not that I know. I've sent her an e-mail, one of many, but she hasn't answered yet. My parents are slowly getting used to the fact of my heritage, but it will take a while for it to sink in.'

'What about you?' she asked, her heart aching all over again for him. 'How are you coping?'

His eyes met hers. 'I feel caught between two very different worlds. The king…' he paused and added with a rueful twist '…I mean, my grandfather, desperately wants me to take up the throne, as do my other relatives I've met, apart from Luca, who seems to be the only one with any real sense of what I'm going through.'

'But you've decided not to take up the throne.'

'I can't turn my back on years of training, Amelia,' he said. 'My adoptive parents sacrificed a lot to get me where I am. Not only that, the patients I've served all these years really mean something to me. If I walk away from the research I've been doing and this new procedure I can't be sure someone else will take up where I left off. I feel I owe it to everyone to carry on the work I'm doing.'

'It's a tough decision,' she said. 'But surely your family will understand…your biological one, I mean.'

He let out a long-winded sigh. 'I'm starting up a fund for the Free Hospital. I thought it was one way I could keep my ties on Niroli without seeming to walk away without some sort of recognition of who I am…or who I was, I suppose I should say.'

'That's a wonderful gesture…. I'm sure much good will come out of it.'

There was a tiny silence broken only by the chirruping of birds in the shrubs nearby.

'Amelia—'

'Alex…I mean, Alessandro…'

He grimaced. 'Please don't call me that.'

'Your Highness?'

'That's even worse,' he said. 'Just call me Alex.'

'Alex, then.' She held out her hand to him. 'I hope you have a good journey home. It was…nice to meet you.'

Alex took her hand in his. 'Amelia…there's something I need to ask you…'

She swallowed at the dark intensity of his eyes as they held hers. 'Yes?'

'When did you know I was the prince?'

Tears burned in the backs of her eyes, but she blinked them back determinedly. She had to let him go, she knew it, but it hurt far more than she could ever have imagined. There was no place for her in his life, not here on Niroli and certainly not in Australia where his family was still trying to get over the shock of his past.

'Answer me, Amelia.' He tightened his hold as she tried to pull away. 'I need to know.'

Her bottom lip started to quiver, but somehow she got it under control as she held his unwavering gaze.

'Did you know who I was before you slept with me that first time?' he asked.

'What difference does it make?'

'Did you sleep with me because I was Alex Hunter or Prince Alessandro?'

'Don't make this any harder for me, Alex,' she begged.

His hold tightened even further. 'Answer me.'

She looked up at him with eyes full of anguish. 'I slept with you because I fell in love with you. I swore I wouldn't be so foolish to fall in love with anyone again, let alone a man who could offer me nothing in return. But I couldn't seem to help myself. I'm sorry….' She brushed at her eyes with the back of her hand. 'I know this is the last thing you need to hear right now…. I won't cause you any trouble. I'm leaving the island so you won't have to see me again.'

'But what if I want to see you again?' he asked. 'What if I told you I was a complete idiot to allow you to walk away from me without telling you how I feel, how I felt from the first moment I saw you, but that I hadn't realised it until the prospect of never seeing you again began to hit home?'

She blinked at him through her tears, her heart leaping in hope. 'Y-you want to see me…some time?'

He smiled one of his lazy smiles. 'I was thinking more along the lines of *all* the time. What do you say, little elf? I know I've asked you this before, but it can't hurt to run it by you one more time. Do you want to run away with me and have my babies?'

Amelia's mouth dropped open. 'I can't believe you said that.'

He grinned down at her. 'That's what you said the last time. I was hoping you might actually believe me this time around. I want you to be my wife. I want you by my side for the rest of my life.'

'You mean…' she swallowed convulsively, her eyes wide and her voice scratchy '…you mean you're not joking?'

He shook his head. 'And to put your mind at ease it didn't just slip out either. I just wanted to make sure you were promising to marry the right guy.'

She looked up at him in growing wonder. 'How do I know if you're the right guy?' she asked as a little smile began to tip up the edges of her mouth.

'Which one of us do you want to marry?' he asked, 'Alex Hunter or His Royal Highness Prince Alessandro Fierezza?'

'I want to marry whichever one loves me the most.'

He kissed the tip of her nose and said, 'Then you've got yourself one hell of a bargain, because we both love you to distraction. Now how's that for a package deal? Are you going to take it or leave it?'

She smiled at him in pure joy and lifted her mouth to meet his. 'I'll take it,' she said.

*As secrets of the past are revealed on Niroli,
a thousand miles away a woman lies dying with
a confession of her own that will rock the royal house....*

'I NEED to see my son.'

The words were weak. The woman was weak. Fragile, yet not the least feeble. Her mind was as sharp as the day she had lied.

'Bring him to me.'

Was it possible, she wondered, to have carried a secret for so long that it could become a part of who she was? For forty years that secret had sat, next to her heart, beating to the rhythm of fear. But she was afraid no longer. In the desert she knew the truth had a way of bubbling to the surface and if it came from lips that were not her own, she would have failed her son a second time.

'Please,' she whispered. 'Bring him to me.'

* * * * *

*Discover how the shock waves of this confession echo, not
only through the desert, but across
the ocean on Niroli, in
BOUGHT BY THE BILLIONAIRE PRINCE,
book three of The Royal House of Niroli.*

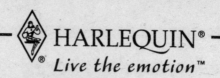

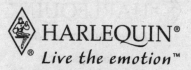

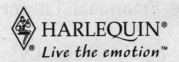

HARLEQUIN®

Super Romance®

...there's more to the story!

Superromance.
A *big* satisfying read about unforgettable
characters. Each month we offer *six* very different
stories that range from family drama to adventure
and mystery, from highly emotional stories to
romantic comedies—and much more! Stories
about people you'll believe in and care about.
Stories too compelling to put down....

Our authors are among today's *best* romance
writers. You'll find familiar names and talented
newcomers. Many of them are award winners—
and you'll see why!

If you want the biggest and best
in romance fiction, you'll get it
from Superromance!

Exciting, Emotional, Unexpected...

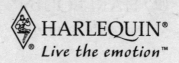

HARLEQUIN®
Live the emotion™

HSDIR06

Harlequin® Historical
Historical Romantic Adventure!

*Imagine a time of chivalrous
knights and unconventional ladies,
roguish rakes and impetuous
heiresses, rugged cowboys
and spirited frontierswomen—
these rich and vivid tales will
capture your imagination!*

*Harlequin Historical...
they're too good to miss!*

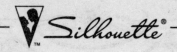

SPECIAL EDITION™

Emotional, compelling stories that capture the intensity of living, loving and creating a family in today's world.

Desire

Modern, passionate reads that are powerful and provocative.

nocturne

Dramatic and sensual tales of paranormal romance.

Romantic SUSPENSE

Romances that are sparked by danger and fueled by passion.

SDIR07